"A SORT OF HUSH FELL OVER MY PREVIOUSLY
BUSY CREATIVE LIFE—NOT A WRITER'S
BLOCK, BUT A SENSE THAT IT WAS TIME TO
STOP GOOFING AROUND WITH A PICK AND
SHOVEL AND GET BEHIND THE CONTROLS OF
ONE BIG GREAT GOD A'MIGHTY
STEAMSHOVEL, A SENSE THAT IT WAS TIME
TO TRY AND DIG SOMETHING BIG OUT OF
THE SAND . . . AND SO, ONE NIGHT . . .
I FOUND MYSELF SITTING AT MY OLD
OFFICE-MODEL UNDERWOOD . . . AND
WRITING THE WORDS THAT BEGIN THIS
STORY: *THE MAN IN BLACK FLED ACROSS THE
DESERT AND THE GUNSLINGER FOLLOWED.*"

—from the Afterword by Stephen King

Turn to the first page and begin the most compulsive
reading experience of our time.

THE
DARK
TOWER

THE GUNSLINGER

STEPHEN KING, one of the bestselling novelists of our time, and
the undisputed master of modern horror, was educated at the
University of Maine at Orono. He lives with his wife Tabitha and
their three children in Bangor, Maine.

THE DARK TOWER

THE GUNSLINGER

by

STEPHEN KING

Illustrated by
Michael Whelan

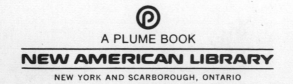

A PLUME BOOK

NEW AMERICAN LIBRARY

NEW YORK AND SCARBOROUGH, ONTARIO

NAL BOOKS ARE AVAILABLE AT QUANTITY DISCOUNTS WHEN USED TO PROMOTE PRODUCTS OR SERVICES. FOR INFORMATION PLEASE WRITE TO PREMIUM MARKETING DIVISION, NEW AMERICAN LIBRARY, 1633 BROADWAY, NEW YORK, NEW YORK 10019.

ACKNOWLEDGMENTS

The Gunslinger, copyright 1978 by Mercury Press, Inc., for *The Magazine of Fantasy and Science Fiction*, October 1978.

The Way Station, copyright 1980 by Mercury Press, Inc., for *The Magazine of Fantasy and Science Fiction*, April 1980.

The Oracle and the Mountains, copyright 1981 by Mercury Press, Inc., for *The Magazine of Fantasy and Science Fiction*, February 1981.

The Slow Mutants, copyright 1981 by Mercury Press, Inc., for *The Magazine of Fantasy and Science Fiction*, July 1981.

The Gunslinger and the Dark Man, copyright 1981 by Mercury Press, Inc., for *The Magazine of Fantasy and Science Fiction*, November 1981.

The Gunslinger previously appeared in a limited edition published by Donald M. Grant, Publisher, Inc., West Kingston, Rhode Island.

Ⓟ

PLUME TRADEMARK REG. U.S. PAT. OFF. AND FOREIGN COUNTRIES
REGISTERED TRADEMARK—MARCA REGISTRADA
HECHO EN OLATHE, KANSAS, U.S.A.

Library of Congress Cataloging-in-Publication Data

King, Stephen, 1947-
   The gunslinger / by Stephen King.
     p.   cm. — (The Dark tower : 1)
   ISBN 0-452-26134-1
   I. Title. II. Series: King, Stephen, 1947-   Dark tower : 1.
PS3561.I483G86 1988
813'.54—dc19
                                            88-9938
                                            CIP

SIGNET, SIGNET CLASSIC, MENTOR, ONYX, PLUME, MERIDIAN and NAL BOOKS are published *in the United States* by NAL PENGUIN INC., 1633 Broadway, New York, New York 10019, *in Canada* by The New American Library of Canada Limited, 81 Mack Avenue, Scarborough, Ontario M1L 1M8

First Plume Printing, September, 1988

1 2 3 4 5 6 7 8 9

PRINTED IN THE UNITED STATES OF AMERICA

CONTENTS

TO
ED FERMAN

who took a chance on these stories,
one by one.

ILLUSTRATIONS

THE
GUNSLINGER

The man in black fled across the desert, and the gunslinger followed.

The desert was the apotheosis of all deserts, huge, standing to the sky for what might have been parsecs in all directions. White; blinding; waterless; without feature save for the faint, cloudy haze of the mountains which sketched themselves on the horizon and the devil-grass which brought sweet dreams, nightmares, death. An occasional tombstone sign pointed the way, for once the drifted track that cut its way through the thick crust of alkali had been a highway and coaches had followed it. The world had moved on since then. The world had emptied.

The gunslinger walked stolidly, not hurrying, not loafing. A hide waterbag was slung around his middle like a bloated sausage. It was almost full. He had progressed through the *khef* over many years, and had reached the fifth level. At the seventh or eighth, he would not have been thirsty; he could have watched his own body dehydrate with clinical, detached attention, watering its crevices and dark inner hollows only when his logic told him it must be done. He was not seventh or eighth. He was fifth. So he was thirsty, although he had no particular urge to drink. In a vague way, all this pleased him. It was romantic.

11

Below the waterbag were his guns, finely weighted to his hand. The two belts crisscrossed above his crotch. The holsters were oiled too deeply for even this Philistine sun to crack. The stocks of the guns were sandalwood, yellow and finely grained. The holsters were tied down with rawhide cord, and they swung heavily against his hips. The brass casings of the cartridges looped into the gunbelts twinkled and flashed and heliographed in the sun. The leather made subtle creaking noises. The guns themselves made no noise. They had spilled blood. There was no need to make noise in the sterility of the desert.

His clothes were the no-color of rain or dust. His shirt was open at the throat, with a rawhide thong dangling loosely in hand-punched eyelets. His pants were seam-stretched dungarees.

He breasted a gently rising dune (although there was no sand here; the desert was hardpan, and even the harsh winds that blew when dark came raised only an aggravating harsh dust like scouring powder) and saw the kicked remains of a tiny campfire on the lee side, the side which the sun would quit earliest. Small signs like this, once more affirming the man in black's essential humanity, never failed to please him. His lips stretched in the pitted, flaked remains of his face. He squatted.

He had burned the devil-grass, of course. It was the only thing out here that *would* burn. It burned with a greasy, flat light, and it burned slow. Border dwellers had told him that devils lived even in the flames. They burned it but would not look into the light. They said the devils hypnotized, beckoned, would eventually draw the one who looked into the fires. And the next man foolish enough to look into the fire might see you.

The burned grass was criss-crossed in the now-familiar ideographic pattern, and crumbled to gray senselessness before the gunslinger's prodding hand. There was nothing in the remains but a charred scrap of bacon, which he ate thoughtfully. It had always been this way. The gunslinger had followed the man in black across the desert for two months now, across the endless, screamingly monotonous purgatorial wastes, and had yet to find spoor other than the hygienic sterile ideographs of the man in black's campfires. He had not found a can, a bottle, or a waterbag (the gunslinger had left four of those behind, like dead snakeskins).

— Perhaps the campfires are a message, spelled out letter by letter. *Take a powder.* Or, *the end draweth nigh.* Or maybe even, *Eat at Joe's.* It didn't matter. He had no understanding of the ideograms, if they were ideograms. And the remains were as cold as all the others. He knew he was closer, but did not know how he knew. That didn't matter either. He stood up, brushing his hands.

No other trace; the wind, razor-sharp, had of course filed away even what scant tracks the hardpan held. He had never even been able to find his quarry's droppings. Nothing. Only these cold campfires along the ancient highway and the relentless range-finder in his own head.

He sat down and allowed himself a short pull from the waterbag. He scanned the desert, looked up at the sun, which was now sliding down the far quadrant of the sky. He got up, removed his gloves from his belt, and began to pull devil-grass for his own fire, which he laid over the ashes the man in black had left. He found the irony, like the romance of his thirst, bitterly appealing.

He did not use the flint and steel until the remains of the day were only the fugitive heat in the ground beneath him and a sardonic orange line on the monochrome western horizon. He watched the south patiently, toward the mountains, not hoping or expecting to see the thin straight line of smoke from a new campfire, but merely watching because that was a part of it. There was nothing. He was close, but only relatively so. Not close enough to see smoke at dusk.

He struck his spark to the dry, shredded grass and lay down upwind, letting the dreamsmoke blow out toward the waste. The wind, except for occasional gyrating dust-devils, was constant.

Above, the stars were unwinking, also constant. Suns and worlds by the million. Dizzying constellations, cold fire in every primary hue. As he watched, the sky washed from violet to ebony. A meteor etched a brief, spectacular arc and winked out. The fire threw strange shadows as the devil-grass burned its slow way down into new patterns — not ideograms but a straightforward crisscross vaguely frightening in its own no-nonsense surety. He had laid his fuel in a pattern that was not artful but only workable. It spoke of blacks and whites. It spoke of a man who might straighten bad pictures in strange hotel rooms. The fire burned its steady, slow flame, and phantoms danced in its incandescent core. The gunslinger did not see. He slept. The two patterns, art and craft, were welded together. The wind moaned. Every now and then a perverse downdraft would make the smoke whirl and eddy toward him, and sporadic whiffs of the smoke touched him. They built dreams in the same way that a small irritant may build a pearl in an oyster. Occasionally the gunslinger moaned with the wind. The stars were as indifferent to this as they were to wars, crucifixions, resurrections. This also would have pleased him.

II

He had come down off the last of the foothills leading the donkey, whose eyes were already dead and bulging with the heat. He had passed the last town three weeks before, and since then there had only been the deserted coach track and an occasional huddle of border dwellers' sod dwellings. The huddles had degenerated into single dwellings, most inhabited by lepers or madmen. He found the madmen better company. One had given him a stainless steel Silva compass and bade him give it to Jesus. The gunslinger took it gravely. If he saw Him, he would turn over the compass. He did not expect to.

Five days had passed since the last hut, and he had begun to suspect there would be no more when he topped the last eroded hill and saw the familiar low-backed sod roof.

The dweller, a surprisingly young man with a wild shock of strawberry hair that reached almost to his waist, was weeding a scrawny stand of corn with zealous abandon. The mule let out a wheezing grunt and the dweller looked up, glaring blue eyes coming target-center on the gunslinger in a moment. He raised both hands in curt salute and then bent to the corn again, humping up the row next to his hut with back bent, tossing devil-grass and an occasional stunted corn plant over his shoulder. His hair flopped and flew in the wind that now came directly from the desert, with nothing to break it.

The gunslinger came down the hill slowly, leading the donkey on which his waterskins sloshed. He paused by the edge of the lifeless-looking cornpatch, drew a drink from one of his skins to start the saliva, and spat into the arid soil.

"Life for your crop."

"Life for your own," the dweller answered and stood up. His back popped audibly. He surveyed the gunslinger without fear. The little of his face visible between beard and hair seemed unmarked by the rot, and his eyes, while a bit wild, seemed sane.

"I don't have anything but corn and beans," he said. "Corn's free, but you'll have to kick something in for the beans. A man brings them out once in a while. He don't stay long." The dweller laughed shortly. "Afraid of spirits."

"I expect he thinks you're one."

"I expect he does."

They looked at each other in silence for a moment.

The dweller put out his hand. "Brown is my name."

The gunslinger shook his hand. As he did so, a scrawny raven croaked from the low peak of the sod roof. The dweller gestured at it briefly:

"That's Zoltan."

At the sound of its name the raven croaked again and flew across to Brown. It landed on the dweller's head and roosted, talons firmly twined in the wild thatch of hair.

"Screw you," Zoltan croaked brightly. "Screw you and the horse you rode in on."

The gunslinger nodded amiably.

"Beans, beans, the musical fruit," the raven recited, inspired. "The more you eat, the more you toot."

"You teach him that?"

"That's all he wants to learn, I guess," Brown said. "Tried to teach him The Lord's Prayer once." His eyes traveled out beyond the hut for a moment, toward the gritty, featureless hardpan. "Guess this ain't Lord's Prayer country. You're a gunslinger. That right?"

"Yes." He hunkered down and brought out his makings. Zoltan launched himself from Brown's head and landed, flittering, on the gunslinger's shoulder.

"After the other one, I guess."

"Yes." The inevitable question formed in his mouth: "How long since he passed by?"

Brown shrugged. "I don't know. Time's funny out here. More than two weeks. Less than two months. The bean man's been twice since he passed. I'd guess six weeks. That's probably wrong."

"The more you eat, the more you toot," Zoltan said.

"Did he stop off?" the gunslinger asked.

Brown nodded. "He stayed supper, same as you will, I guess. We passed the time."

The gunslinger stood up and the bird flew back to the roof, squawking. He felt an odd, trembling eagerness. "What did he talk about?"

Brown cocked an eyebrow at him. "Not much. Did it ever rain and when did I come here and had I buried my wife. I did most of the talking, which ain't usual." He paused, and the only sound was the stark wind. "He's a sorcerer, ain't he?"

"Yes."

Brown nodded slowly. "I knew. Are you?"

"I'm just a man."

"You'll never catch him."

"I'll catch him."

They looked at each other, a sudden depth of feeling between them, the dweller upon his dust-puff-dry ground, the gunslinger on the hardpan that shelved down to the desert. He reached for his flint.

"Here." Brown produced a sulfur-headed match and struck it with a grimed nail. The gunslinger pushed the tip of his smoke into the flame and drew.

"Thanks."

"You'll want to fill your skins," the dweller said, turning away. "Spring's under the eaves in back. I'll start dinner."

The gunslinger stepped gingerly over the rows of corn and went around back. The spring was at the bottom of a hand-dug well, lined with stones to keep the powdery earth from caving. As he descended the rickety ladder, the gunslinger reflected that the stones must represent two years' work easily — hauling, dragging, laying. The water was clear but slow-moving, and filling the skins was a long chore.

While he was topping the second, Zoltan perched on the lip of the well.

"Screw you and the horse you rode in on," he advised.

He looked up, startled. The shaft was about fifteen feet deep: easy enough for Brown to drop a rock on him, break his head, and steal everything on him. A crazy or a rotter wouldn't do it; Brown was neither. Yet he liked Brown, and so he pushed the thought out of his mind and got the rest of his water. What came, came.

When he came through the hut's door and walked down the steps (the hovel proper was set below ground level, designed to catch and hold the coolness of the nights), Brown was poking ears of corn into the embers of a tiny fire with a hardwood spatula. Two ragged plates had been set at opposite ends of a dun blanket. Water for the beans was just beginning to bubble in a pot hung over the fire.

"I'll pay for the water, too."

Brown did not look up. "The water's a gift from God. Pappa Doc brings the beans."

The gunslinger grunted a laugh and sat down with his back against one rude wall, folded his arms and closed his eyes. After a little, the smell of roasting corn came to his nose. There was a pebbly rattle as Brown dumped a paper of dry beans into the pot. An occasional *tak-tak-tak* as Zoltan walked restlessly on the roof. He was tired; he had been going sixteen and sometimes eighteen hours a day between here and the horror that had occurred in Tull, the last village. And he had been afoot for the last twelve days; the mule was at the end of its endurance.

Tak-tak-tak.

Two weeks, Brown had said, or as much as six. Didn't matter. There had been calendars in Tull, and they had remembered the man in black because of the old man he had healed on his way through. Just an old man dying with the weed. An old man of thirty-five. And if Brown was right, the man in black had lost ground since then. But the desert was next. And the desert would be hell.

Tak-tak-tak.

— Lend me your wings, bird. I'll spread them and fly on the thermals.

He slept.

III

Brown woke him up five hours later. It was dark. The only light was the dull cherry glare of the banked embers.

"Your mule has passed on," Brown said. "Dinner's ready."

"How?"

Brown shrugged. "Roasted and boiled, how else? You picky?"

"No, the mule."

"It just laid over, that's all. It looked like an old mule." And with a touch of apology: "Zoltan et the eyes."

"Oh." He might have expected it. "All right."

Brown surprised him again when they sat down to the blanket that served as a table by asking a brief blessing: Rain, health, expansion to the spirit.

"Do you believe in an afterlife?" The gunslinger asked him as Brown dropped three ears of hot corn onto his plate.

Brown nodded. "I think this is it."

IV

The beans were like bullets, the corn tough. Outside, the prevailing wind snuffled and whined around the ground-level eaves. He ate quickly, ravenously, drinking four cups of water with the meal. Halfway through, there was a machine-gun rapping at the door. Brown got up and let Zoltan in. The bird flew across the room and hunched moodily in the corner.

"Musical fruit," he muttered.

After dinner, the gunslinger offered his tobacco.

— Now. Now the questions will come.

But Brown asked no questions. He smoked and looked at the dying embers of the fire. It was already noticeably cooler in the hovel.

"Lead us not into temptation," Zoltan said suddenly, apocalyptically.

The gunslinger started as if he had been shot at. He was suddenly sure that it was an illusion, all of it (not a dream, no; an enchantment), that the man in black had spun a spell and was trying to tell him something in a maddeningly obtuse, symbolic way.

"Have you been through Tull?" he asked suddenly.

Brown nodded. "Coming here, and once to sell corn. It rained that year. Lasted maybe fifteen minutes. The ground just seemed to open and suck it up. An hour later it was just as white and dry as ever. But the corn — God, the corn. You could see it grow. That wasn't so bad. But you could *hear* it, as if the rain had given it a mouth. It wasn't a happy sound. It seemed to be sighing and groaning its way out of the earth." He paused. "I had extra, so I took it and sold it. Pappa Doc said he'd do it, but he would have cheated me. So I went."

"You don't like town?"

"No."

"I almost got killed there," the gunslinger said abruptly.

"That so?"

"I killed a man that was touched by God," the gunslinger said. "Only it wasn't God. It was the man in black."

"He laid you a trap."

"Yes."

The looked at each other across the shadows, the moment taking on overtones of finality.

— *Now* the questions will come.

But Brown had nothing to say. His smoke was a smoldering roach, but when the gunslinger tapped his poke, Brown shook his head.

Zoltan shifted restlessly, seemed about to speak, subsided.

"May I tell you about it?" the gunslinger asked.

"Sure."

The gunslinger searched for words to begin and found none. "I have to flow," he said.

Brown nodded. "The water does that. The corn, please?"

"Sure."

He went up the stairs and out into the dark. The stars glittered overhead in a mad splash. The wind pulsed steadily. His urine arched out over the powdery cornfield in a wavering stream. The man in black had sent him here. Brown might even be the man in black himself. It might be —

He shut the thoughts away. The only contingency he had not learned how to bear was the possibility of his own madness. He went back inside.

"Have you decided if I'm an enchantment yet?" Brown asked, amused.

The gunslinger paused on the tiny landing, startled. Then he came down slowly and sat.

"I started to tell you about Tull."

"Is it growing?"

"It's dead," the gunslinger said, and the words hung in the air.

Brown nodded. "The desert. I think it may strangle

everything eventually. Did you know that there was once a coach road across the desert?"

The gunslinger closed his eyes. His mind whirled crazily.

"You doped me," he said thickly.

"No. I've done nothing."

The gunslinger opened his eyes warily.

"You won't feel right about it unless I invite you," Brown said. "And so I do. Will you tell me about Tull?"

The gunslinger opened his mouth hesitantly and was surprised to find that this time the words were there. He began to speak in flat bursts that slowly spread into an even, slightly toneless narrative. The doped feeling left him, and he found himself oddly excited. He talked deep into the night. Brown did not interrupt at all. Neither did the bird.

V

He had bought the mule in Pricetown, and when he reached Tull, it was still fresh. The sun had set an hour earlier, but the gunslinger had continued traveling, guided by the town glow in the sky, then by the uncannily clear notes of a honky-tonk piano playing *Hey Jude*. The road widened as it took on tributaries.

The forests had been gone long now, replaced by the monotonous flat country: endless, desolate fields gone to timothy and low shrubs, shacks, eerie, deserted estates guarded by brooding, shadowed mansions where demons undeniably walked; leering, empty shanties where the people had either moved on or had been moved along, an occasional dweller's hovel, given away by a single flickering point of light in the dark, or by sullen, inbred clans toiling silently in the fields by day. Corn was the main crop, but there were beans and also some peas. An occasional scrawny cow stared at him lumpishly from between peeled alder poles. Coaches had passed him four times, twice coming and twice going, nearly empty as they came up on him from behind and bypassed him and his mule, fuller as they headed back toward the forests of the north.

It was ugly country. It had showered twice since he had left Pricetown, grudgingly both times. Even the timothy looked yellow and dispirited. Ugly country. He had seen no sign of the man in black. Perhaps he had taken a coach.

The road made a bend, and beyond it the gunslinger clucked the mule to a stop and looked down at Tull. It was at the floor of a circular, bowl-shaped hollow, a shoddy jewel in a cheap setting. There were a number of lights, most of them clustered around the area of the music. There looked to be four streets, three running at right angles to the coach road, which was the main avenue of the town. Perhaps there would be a restaurant. He doubted it, but perhaps. He clucked at the mule.

More houses sporadically lined the road now, most of them still deserted. He passed a tiny graveyard with moldy, leaning wooden slabs overgrown and choked by the rank devil-grass. Perhaps five hundred feet further on he passed a chewed sign which said: TULL

The paint was flaked almost to the point of illegibility. There was another further on, but the gunslinger was not able to read that one at all.

A fool's chorus of half-stoned voices was rising in the final protracted lyric of *Hey Jude* — "Naa-naa-naa naa-na-na-na . . . hey, Jude . . . " — as he entered the town proper. It was a dead sound, like the wind in the hollow of a rotted tree. Only the prosaic thump and pound of the honky-tonk piano saved him from seriously wondering if the man in black might not have raised ghosts to inhabit a deserted town. He smiled a little at the thought.

There were a few people on the streets, not many, but a few. Three ladies wearing black slacks and identical middy blouses passed by on the opposite boardwalk, not looking at him with pointed curiosity. Their faces seemed to swim above their all-but-invisible bodies like huge, pallid baseballs with eyes. A solemn old man with a straw hat perched firmly on top of his head watched him from the steps of a boarded-up grocery store. A scrawny tailor with a late customer paused to watch him by; he held up the lamp in his window for a better look. The gunslinger nodded. Neither the tailor nor his customer nodded back. He could feel their eyes resting heavily against the low-slung holsters that lay against his hips. A young boy, perhaps thirteen, and his girl crossed the street a block up, pausing imperceptibly. Their footfalls raised little hanging clouds of dust. A few of the streetside lamps worked, but their glass sides were cloudy with congealed oil. Most had been crashed out. There was a livery, probably depending on the coach line for its survival. Three boys were crouched silently around a marble ring drawn in the dust to one side of the barn's gaping maw, smoking cornshuck cigarettes. They made long shadows in the yard.

The gunslinger led his mule past them and looked into the dim depths of the barn. One lamp glowed sunkenly, and a shadow jumped and flickered as a gangling old man in bib overalls forked loose timothy hay into the hay loft with huge, grunting swipes of his fork.

"Hey!" the gunslinger called.

The fork faltered and the hostler looked around waspishly. "Hey yourself!"

"I got a mule here."

"Good for you."

The gunslinger flicked a heavy, unevenly milled gold

piece into the semidark. It rang on the old, chaff-drifted boards and glittered.

The hostler came forward, bent, picked it up, squinted at the gunslinger. His eyes dropped to the gunbelts and he nodded sourly.

"How long you want him put up?"

"A night. Maybe two. Maybe longer."

"I ain't got no change for gold."

"I'm not asking for any."

"Blood money," the hostler muttered.

"What?"

"Nothing." The hostler caught the mule's bridle and led him inside.

"Rub him down!" the gunslinger called. The old man did not turn.

The gunslinger walked out to the boys crouched around the marble ring. They had watched the entire exchange with contemptuous interest.

"How they hanging?" the gunslinger asked conversationally.

No answer.

"You dudes live in town?"

No answer.

One of the boys removed a crazily tilted twist of corn-shuck from his mouth, grasped a green cat's-eye marble, and squirted it into the dirt circle. It struck a croaker and knocked it outside. He picked up the cat's-eye and prepared to shoot again.

"There a restaurant in this town?" the gunslinger asked.

One of them looked up, the youngest. There was a huge cold-sore at the corner of his mouth, but his eyes were still ingenuous. He looked at the gunslinger with hooded brimming wonder that was touching and frightening.

"Might get a burger at Sheb's."

"That the honky-tonk?"

The boy nodded but didn't speak. The eyes of his playmates had turned ugly and hostile.

The gunslinger touched the brim of his hat. "I'm grateful. It's good to know someone in this town is bright enough to talk."

He walked past, mounted the boardwalk and started down toward Sheb's, hearing the clear, contemptuous voice of one of the others, hardly more than a childish treble: "Weed-eater! How long you been screwin' your sister, Charlie? Weed-eater!"

There were three flaring kerosene lamps in front of Sheb's, one to each side and one nailed above the drunk-hung batwing doors. The chorus of *Hey Jude* had petered out, and the piano was plinking some other old ballad. Voices murmured like broken threads. The gunslinger paused outside for a moment, looking in. Sawdust floor, spittoons by the tipsy-legged tables. A plank bar on saw-horses. A gummy mirror behind it, reflecting the piano player, who wore an inevitable piano-stool slouch. The front of the piano had been removed so you could watch the wooden keys whonk up and down as the contraption was played. The bartender was a straw-haired woman wearing a dirty blue dress. One strap was held with a safety pin. There were perhaps six townies in the back of the room, juicing and playing Watch Me apathetically. Another half-dozen were grouped loosely about the piano. Four or five at the bar. And an old man with wild gray hair collapsed at a table by the doors. The gunslinger went in.

Heads swiveled to look at him and his guns. There was a moment of near silence, except for the oblivious piano player, who continued to tinkle. Then the woman mopped at the bar, and things shifted back.

"Watch me," one of the players in the corner said and matched three hearts with four spades, emptying his hand. The one with the hearts swore, handed over his bet, and the next was dealt.

The gunslinger approached the bar. "You got hamburger?" he asked.

"Sure." She looked him in the eye, and she might have been pretty when she started out, but now her face was lumpy and there was a livid scar corkscrewed across her forehead. She had powdered it heavily, but it called attention rather than camouflaging. "It's dear, though."

"I figured. Gimme three burgers and a beer."

Again that subtle shift in tone. Three hamburgers. Mouths watered and tongues liked at saliva with slow lust. Three hamburgers.

"That would go you five bucks. With the beer."

The gunslinger put a gold piece on the bar.

Eyes followed it.

There was a sullenly smoldering charcoal brazier behind the bar and to the left of the mirror. The woman disappeared into a small room behind it and returned with meat on a paper. She scrimped out three patties and put them on the fire. The smell that arose was maddening. The gunslinger stood with stolid indifference, only peripherally aware of the faltering piano, the slowing of the card game, the sidelong glances of the barflies.

The man was halfway up behind him when the gunslinger saw him in the mirror. The man was almost completely bald, and his hand was wrapped around the haft of a gigantic hunting knife that was looped onto his belt like a holster.

"Go sit down," the gunslinger said quietly.

The man stopped. His upper lip lifted unconsciously, like a dog's, and there was a moment of silence. Then he went back to his table, and the atmosphere shifted back again.

His beer came in a cracked glass schooner. "I ain't got change for gold," the woman said truculently.

"Don't expect any."

She nodded angrily, as if this show of wealth, even at her benefit, incensed her. But she took his gold, and a moment later the hamburgers came on a cloudy plate, still red around the edges.

"Do you have salt?"

She gave it to him from underneath the bar. "Bread?"

"No." He knew she was lying, but he didn't push it. The bald man was staring at him with cyanosed eyes, his hands clenching and unclenching on the splintered and gouged surface of his table. His nostrils flared with pulsating regularity.

The gunslinger began to eat steadily, almost blandly, chopping the meat apart and forking it into his mouth, trying not to think of what might have been added to cut the beef.

He was almost through, ready to call for another beer and roll a smoke when the hand fell on his shoulder.

He suddenly became aware that the room had gone silent again, and he tasted thick tension in the air. He turned around and stared into the face of the man who had been asleep by the door when he entered. It was a terrible face. The odor of the devil-grass was a rank miasma. The eyes were damned, the staring, glaring eyes of those who see but do not see, eyes ever turned inward to the sterile hell of dreams beyond control, dreams unleashed, risen out of the stinking swamps of the unconscious.

The woman behind the bar made a small moaning sound.

The cracked lips writhed, lifted, revealing the green,

mossy teeth, and the gunslinger thought: — He's not even smoking it anymore. He's chewing it. He's really *chewing* it.

And on the heels of that: — He's a dead man. He should have been dead a year ago.

And on the heels of that: — The man in black.

They stared at each other, the gunslinger and the man who had gone around the rim of madness.

He spoke, and the gunslinger, dumfounded, heard himself addressed in the High Speech:

"The gold for a favor, gunslinger. Just one? For a pretty."

The High Speech. For a moment his mind refused to track it. It had been years — God! — centuries, millenniums; there was no more High Speech, he was the last, the last gunslinger. The others were —

Numbed, he reached into his breast pocket and produced a gold piece. The split, scrabbed hand reached for it, fondled it, held it up to reflect the greasy glare of the kerosene lamps. It threw off its proud civilized glow; golden, reddish, bloody.

"Ahhhhhh . . . " An inarticulate sound of pleasure. The old man did a weaving turn and began moving back to his table, holding the coin at eye level, turning it, flashing it.

The room was emptying rapidly, the batwings shuttling madly back and forth. The piano player closed the lid of his instrument with a bang and exited after the others in long, comic-opera strides.

"Sheb!" The woman screamed after him, her voice an odd mixture of fear and shrewishness, "Sheb, you come back here! Goddammit!"

The old man, meanwhile, had gone back to his table.

He spun the gold piece on the gouged wood, and the dead-alive eyes followed it with empty fascination. He spun it a second time, a third, and his eyelids drooped. The fourth time, and his head settled to the wood before the coin stopped.

"There," she said softly, furiously. "You've driven out my trade. Are you satisfied?"

"They'll be back," the gunslinger said.

"Not tonight they won't."

"Who is he?" He gestured at the weed-eater.

"Go — " She completed the command by describing an impossible act of masturbation.

"I have to know," the gunslinger said patiently. "He — "

"He talked to you funny," she said. "Nort never talked like that in his life."

"I'm looking for a man. You would know him."

She stared at him, the anger dying. It was replaced with speculation, then with a high, wet gleam that he had seen before. The rickety building ticked thoughtfully to itself. A dog barked brayingly, far away. The gunslinger waited. She saw his knowledge and the gleam was replaced by hopelessness, by a dumb need that had no mouth.

"You know my price," she said.

He looked at her steadily. The scar would not show in the dark. Her body was lean enough so the desert and grit and grind hadn't been able to sag everything. And she'd once been pretty, maybe even beautiful. Not that it mattered. It would not have mattered if the grave-beetles had nested in the arid blackness of her womb. It had all been written.

Her hands came up to her face and there was still some juice left in her — enough to weep.

"Don't *look!* You don't have to look at me so mean!"

"I'm sorry," the gunslinger said. "I didn't mean to be mean."

"None of you mean it!" She cried at him.

"Put out the lights."

She wept, hands at her face. He was glad she had her hands at her face. Not because of the scar but because it gave her back her maidenhood, if not head. The pin that held the strap of her dress glittered in the greasy light.

"Put out the lights and lock up. Will he steal anything?"

"No," she whispered.

"Then put out the lights."

She would not remove her hands until she was behind him and she doused the lamps one by one, turning down the wicks and then breathing the flames into extinction. Then she took his hand in the dark and it was warm. She led him upstairs. There was no light to hide their act.

VI

He made cigarettes in the dark, then lit them and passed one to her. The room held her scent, fresh lilac, pathetic. The smell of the desert had overlaid it, crippled it. It was like the smell of the sea. He realized he was afraid of the desert ahead.

"His name is Nort," she said. No harshness had been worn out of her voice. "Just Nort. He died."

The gunslinger waited.

"He was touched by God."

The gunslinger said, "I have never seen Him."

"He was here ever since I can remember — Nort, I mean, not God." She laughed jaggedly into the dark. "He had a honeywagon for a while. Started to drink. Started to smell the grass. Then to smoke it. The kids started to follow him around and sic their dogs onto him. He wore old green pants that stank. Do you understand?"

"Yes."

"He started to chew it. At the last he just sat in there and didn't eat anything. He might have been a king, in his mind. The children might have been his jesters, and the dogs his princes."

"Yes."

"He died right in front of this place," she said. "He came clumping down the boardwalk — his boots wouldn't wear out, they were engineer boots — with the children and dogs behind him. He looked like wire clothes hangers all wrapped and twirled together. You could see all the lights of hell in his eyes, but he was grinning, just like the grins the children carve into their pumpkins on All-Saints Eve. You could smell the dirt and the rot and the weed. It was running down from the corners of his mouth like green blood. I think he meant to come in and listen to Sheb play the piano. And right in front, he stopped and cocked his head. I could see him, and I thought he heard a coach, although there was none due. Then he puked, and it was black and full of blood. It went right through that grin like sewer water through a grate. The stink was enough to make you want to run mad. He raised up his arms and just threw over. That was all. He died with that grin on his face, in his own vomit."

She was trembling beside him. Outside, the wind kept up its steady whine, and somewhere far away a door was banging, like a sound heard in a dream. Mice ran in the walls. The gunslinger thought in the back of his mind that it was probably the only place in town prosperous enough to support mice. He put a hand on her belly and she started violently, then relaxed.

"The man in black," he said.

"You have to have it, don't you!"

"Yes."

"All right. I'll tell you." She grasped his hand in both of hers and told him.

VII

He came in the late afternoon of the day Nort died, and the wind was whooping up, pulling away the loose topsoil, sending sheets of grit and uprooted stalks of corn windmilling past. Kennerly had padlocked the livery, and the other few merchants had shuttered their windows and laid boards across the shutters. The sky was the yellow color of old cheese and the clouds moved flyingly across it, as if they had seen something horrifying in the desert wastes where they had so lately been.

He came in a rickety rig with a rippling tarp tied across its bed. They watched him come, and old man Kennerly, lying by the window with a bottle in one hand and the loose, hot flesh of his second-eldest daughter's left breast in the other, resolved not to be there if he should knock.

But the man in black went by without hawing the bay that pulled his rig, and the spinning wheels spumed up dust that the wind clutched eagerly. He might have been a priest or a monk; he wore a black cassock that had been floured with dust, and a loose hood covered his head and obscured his features. It rippled and flapped. Beneath the garment's hem, heavy buckled boots with square toes.

He pulled up in front of Sheb's and tethered the horse, which lowered its head and grunted at the ground. Around the back of the rig he untied one flap, found a weathered saddlebag, threw it over his shoulder, and went in through the batwings.

Alice watched him curiously, but no one else noticed

his arrival. The rest were drunk as lords. Sheb was playing Methodist hymns ragtime, and the grizzled layabouts
who had come in early to avoid the storm and to attend
Nort's wake had sung themselves hoarse. Sheb, drunk
nearly to the point of senselessness, intoxicated and horny
with his own continued existence, played with hectic, shut-
tlecock speed, fingers flying like looms.

Voices screeched and hollered, never overcoming the
wind but sometimes seeming to challenge it. In the corner
Zachary had thrown Amy Feldon's skirts over her head and
was painting zodiac signs on her knees. A few other women
circulated. A fervid glow seemed to be on all of them. The
dull stormglow that filtered through the batwings seemed
to mock them, however.

Nort had been laid out on two tables in the center of
the room. His boots made a mystical V. His mouth hung
open in a slack grin, although someone had closed his eyes
and put slugs on them. His hands had been folded on his
chest with a sprig of devil-grass in them. He smelled like
poison.

The man in black pushed back his hood and came to
the bar. Alice watched him, feeling trepidation mixed with
the familiar want that hid within her. There was no religious symbol on him, although that meant nothing by itself.

"Whiskey," he said. His voice was soft and pleasant.
"Good whiskey."

She reached under the counter and brought out a bottle
of Star. She could have palmed off the local popskull on
him as her best, but did not. She poured, and the man in
black watched her. His eyes were large, luminous. The
shadows were too thick to determine their color exactly.
Her need intensified. The hollering and whooping went
on behind, unabated. Sheb, the worthless gelding, was
playing about the Christian Soldiers and somebody had
persuaded Aunt Mill to sing. Her voice, warped and dis-

torted, cut through the babble like a dull ax through a calf's brain.

"Hey, Allie!"

She went to serve, resentful of the stranger's silence, resentful of his no-color eyes and her own restless groin. She was afraid of her needs. They were capricious and beyond her control. They might be the signal of the change, which would in turn signal the beginning of her old age — a condition which in Tull was usually as short and bitter as a winter sunset.

She drew beer until the keg was empty, then broached another. She knew better than to ask Sheb; he would come willingly enough, like the dog he was, and would either chop off his own fingers or spume beer all over everything. The stranger's eyes were on her as she went about it; she could feel them.

"It's busy," he said when she returned. He had not touched his drink, merely rolled it between his palms to warm it.

"Wake," she said.

"I noticed the departed."

"They're bums," she said with sudden hatred. "All bums."

"It excites them. He's dead. They're not."

"He was their butt when he was alive. It's not right that he should be their butt now. It's . . . " She trailed off, not able to express what it was, or how it was obscene.

"Weed-eater?"

"Yes! What else did he have?"

Her tone was accusing, but he did not drop his eyes, and she felt the blood rush to her face. "I'm sorry. Are you a priest? This must revolt you."

"I'm not and it doesn't." He knocked the whiskey back neatly and did not grimace. "Once more, please."

"I'll have to see the color of your coin first. I'm sorry."

"No need to be."

He put a rough silver coin on the counter, thick on one edge, thin on the other, and she said as she would say later: "I don't have change for this."

He shook his head, dismissing it, and watched absently as he poured again.

"Are you only passing through?" she asked.

He did not reply for a long time, and she was about to repeat when he shook his head impatiently. "Don't talk trivialities. You're here with death."

She recoiled, hurt and amazed, her first thought being that he had lied about his holiness to test her.

"You cared for him," he said flatly. "Isn't that true?"

"Who? Nort?" She laughed, affecting annoyance to cover her confusion. "I think you better — "

"You're soft-hearted and a little afraid," he went on, "and he was on the weed, looking out hell's back door. And there he is, and they've even slammed the door now, and you don't think they'll open it until it's time for you to walk through, isn't it so?"

"What are you, drunk?"

"Mistuh Norton, he dead," the man in black intoned sardonically. "Dead as anybody. Dead as you or anybody."

"Get out of my place." She felt a trembling loathing spring up in her, but the warmth still radiated from her belly.

"It's all right," he said softly. "It's all right. Wait. Just wait."

The eyes were blue. She felt suddenly easy in her mind, as if she had taken a drug.

"See?" he asked her. "Do you see?"

She nodded dumbly and he laughed aloud — a fine, strong, untainted laugh that swung heads around. He whirled and faced them, suddenly made the center of attention by some unknown alchemy. Aunt Mill faltered and

subsided, leaving a cracked high note bleeding on the air.
Sheb struck a discord and halted. They looked at the stranger
uneasily. Sand rattled against the sides of the building.

The silence held, spun itself out. Her breath had clogged in her throat and she looked down and saw both hands
pressed to her belly beneath the bar. They all looked at
him and he looked at them. Then the laugh burst forth again,
strong, rich, beyond denial. But there was no urge to laugh
along with him.

"I'll show you a wonder!" he cried at them. But they
only watched him, like obedient children taken to see a
magician in whom they have grown too old to believe.

The man in black sprang forward, and Aunt Mill drew
away from him. He grinned fiercely and slapped her broad
belly. A short, unwitting cackle was forced out of her, and
the man in black threw back his head.

"It's better, isn't it?"

Aunt Mill cackled again, suddenly broke into sobs, and
fled blindly through the doors. The others watched her go
silently. The storm was beginning; shadows followed each
other, rising and falling on the white cyclorama of the sky.
A man near the piano with a forgotten beer in one hand
made a groaning, grinning sound.

The man in black stood over Nort, grinning down at
him. The wind howled and shrieked and thrummed. Something large struck the side of the building and bounced
away. One of the men at the bar tore himself free and exited
in looping, grotesque strides. Thunder racketed in sudden
dry vollies.

"All right," the man in black grinned. "All right, let's
get down to it."

He began to spit into Nort's face, aiming carefully. The
spittle gleamed on his forehead, pearled down the shaven
beak of his nose.

Under the bar, her hands worked faster.

Sheb laughed, loon-like, and hunched over. He began to cough up phlegm, huge and sticky gobs of it, and let fly. The man in black roared approval and pounded him on the back. Sheb grinned, one gold tooth twinkling.

Some fled. Others gathered in a loose ring around Nort. His face and the dewlapped rooster-wrinkles of his neck and upper chest gleamed with liquid — liquid so precious in this dry country. And suddenly it stopped, as if on signal. There was ragged, heavy breathing.

The man in black suddenly lunged across the body, jackknifing over it in a smooth arc. It was pretty, like a flash of water. He caught himself on his hands, sprang to his feet in a twist, grinning, and went over again. One of the watchers forgot himself, began to applaud, and suddenly backed away, eyes cloudy with terror. He slobbered a hand across his mouth and made for the door.

Nort twitched the third time the man in black went across.

A sound went through the watchers — a grunt — and then they were silent. The man in black threw his head back and howled. His chest moved in a quick, shallow rhythm as he sucked air. He began to go back and forth at a faster clip, pouring over Nort's body like water poured from one glass to another glass. The only sound in the room was the tearing rasp of his respiration and the rising pulse of the storm.

Nort drew a deep, dry breath. His hands rattled and pounded aimlessly on the table. Sheb screeched and exited. One of the women followed him.

The man in black went across once more, twice, thrice. The whole body was vibrating now, trembling and rapping and twitching. The smell of rot and excrement and decay billowed up in choking waves. His eyes opened.

Alice felt her feet propelling her backward. She struck the mirror, making it shiver, and blind panic took over. She bolted like a steer.

"I've given it to you," the man in black called after her, panting. "Now you can sleep easy. Even *that* isn't irreversible. Although it's . . . so . . . goddamned . . . *funny!*" And he began to laugh again. The sound faded as she raced up the stairs, not stopping until the door to the three rooms above the bar was bolted.

She began to giggle then, rocking back and forth on her haunches by the door. The sound rose to a keening wail that mixed with the wind.

Downstairs, Nort wandered absently out into the storm to pull some weed. The man in black, now the only patron of the bar, watched him go, still grinning.

When she forced herself to go back down that evening, carrying a lamp in one hand and a heavy stick of stovewood in the other, the man in black was gone, rig and all. But Nort was there, sitting at the table by the door as if he had never been away. The smell of the weed was on him, but not as heavily as she might have expected.

He looked up at her and smiled tentatively. "Hello, Allie."

"Hello, Nort." She put the stovewood down and began lighting the lamps, not turning her back to him.

"I been touched by God," he said presently. "I ain't going to die no more. He said so. It was a promise."

"How nice for you, Nort." The spill she was holding dropped through her trembling fingers and she picked it up.

"I'd like to stop chewing the grass," he said. "I don't enjoy it no more. It don't seem right for a man touched by God to be chewing the weed."

"Then why don't you stop?"

Her exasperation startled her into looking at him as a man again, rather than an infernal miracle. What she saw was a rather sad-looking specimen only half-stoned, looking hangdog and ashamed. She could not be frightened by him anymore.

"I shake," he said. "And I want it. I can't stop. Allie, you was always so good to me — " he began to weep. "I can't even stop peeing myself."

She walked to the table and hesitated there, uncertain.

"He could have made me not want it," he said through the tears. "He could have done that if he could have made me be alive. I ain't complaining . . . I don't want to complain . . . " He stared around hauntedly and whispered, "He might strike me dead if I did."

"Maybe it's a joke. He seemd to have quite a sense of humor."

Nort took his poke from where it dangled inside his shirt and brought out a handful of grass. Unthinkingly she knocked it away and then drew her hand back, horrified.

"I can't help it, Allie, I can't — " and he made a crippled dive for the poke. She could have stopped him, but she made no effort. She went back to lighting the lamps, tired although the evening had barely begun. But nobody came in that night except old man Kennerly, who had missed everything. He did not seem particularly surprised to see Nort. He ordered beer, asked where Sheb was, and pawed her. The next day things were almost normal, although none of the children followed Nort. The day after that, the catcalls resumed. Life had gotten back on its own sweet keel. The uprooted corn was gathered together by the children, and a week after Nort's resurrection, they burned it in the middle of the street. The fire was momentarily bright and most of the barflies stepped or staggered out to watch. They looked primitive. Their faces seemed to float between the flames and the ice-chip brilliance of the sky. Allie watched them and felt a pang of fleeting despair for the sad times of the world. Things had stretched apart. There was no glue at the center of things anymore. She had never seen the ocean, never would.

"If I had *guts*," she murmured, "If I had guts, guts, *guts* . . . "

Nort raised his head at the sound of her voice and smiled emptily at her from hell. She had no guts. Only a bar and a scar.

The fire burned down rapidly and her customers came back in. She began to dose herself with the Star Whiskey, and by midnight she was blackly drunk.

VIII

She ceased her narrative, and when he made no immediate comment, she thought at first that the story had put him to sleep. She had begun to drowse herself when he asked: "That's all?"

"Yes. That's all. It's very late."

"Um." He was rolling another cigarette.

"Don't go getting your tobacco dandruff in my bed," she told him, more sharply than she had intended.

"No."

Silence again. The tip of his cigarette winked off and on.

"You'll be leaving in the morning," she said dully.

"I should. I think he's left a trap for me here."

"Don't go," she said.

"We'll see."

He turned on his side away from her, but she was comforted. He would stay. She drowsed.

On the edge of sleep she thought again about the way Nort had addressed him, in that strange talk. She had not seen him express emotion before or since. Even his love-making had been a silent thing, and only at the last had his breathing roughened and then stopped for a minute. He was like something out of a fairytale or a myth, the last of his breed in a world that was writing the last page of its book. It didn't matter. He would stay for a while. Tomorrow was time enough to think, or the day after that. She slept.

IX

In the morning she cooked him grits which he ate without comment. He shoveled them into his mouth without thinking about her, hardly seeing her. He knew he should go. Every minute he sat here the man in black was further away — probably into the desert by now. His path had been undeviatingly south.

"Do you have a map?" he asked suddenly, looking up.

"Of the town?" she laughed. "There isn't enough of it to need a map."

"No. Of what's south of here."

Her smile faded. "The desert. Just the desert. I thought you'd stay for a little."

"What's south of the desert?"

"How would I know? Nobody crosses it. Nobody's tried since I was here." She wiped her hands on her apron, got potholders, and dumped the tub of water she had been heating into the sink, where it splashed and steamed.

He got up.

"Where are you going?" She heard the shrill fear in her voice and hated it.

"To the stable. If anyone knows, the hostler will." He

put his hands on her shoulders. The hands were warm. "And to arrange for my mule. If I'm going to be here, he should be taken care of. For when I leave."

But not yet. She looked up at him. "But you watch that Kennerly. If he doesn't know a thing, he'll make it up."

When he left she turned to the sink, feeling the hot, warm drift of her grateful tears.

X

Kennerly was toothless, unpleasant, and plagued with daughters. Two half-grown ones peeked at the gunslinger from the dusty shadows of the barn. A baby drooled happily in the dirt. A full-grown one, blonde, dirty, sensual, watched with a speculative curiosity as she drew water from the groaning pump beside the building.

The hostler met him halfway between the door to his establishment and the street. His manner vacillated between hostility and a craven sort of fawning — like a stud mongrel that has been kicked too often.

"It's bein' cared for," he said, and before the gunslinger could reply, Kennerly turned on his daughter: "You get in, Soobie! You get right the hell in!"

Soobie began to drag her bucket sullenly toward the shack appended to the barn.

"You meant my mule," the gunslinger said.

"Yes, sir. Ain't seen a mule in quite a time. Time was they used to grow up wild for want of 'em, but the world has moved on. Ain't seen nothin' but a few oxen and the coach horses and . . . Soobie, I'll whale you, 'fore God!"

"I don't bite," the gunslinger said pleasantly.

Kennerly cringed a little. "It ain't you. No, sir, it ain't *you.*" He grinned loosely. "She's just naturally gawky.·

She's got a devil. She's wild." His eyes darkened. "It's coming to Last Times, mister. You know how it says in the Book. Children won't obey their parents, and a plague'll be visited on the multitudes."

The gunslinger nodded, then pointed south. "What's out there?"

Kennerly grinned again, showing gums and a few sociable yellow teeth. "Dwellers. Weed. Desert. What else?" He cackled, and his eyes measured the gunslinger coldly.

"How big is the desert?"

"Big." Kennerly endeavored to look serious. "Maybe three hundred miles. Maybe a thousand. I can't tell you, mister. There's nothing out there but devil-grass and maybe demons. That's the way the other fella went. The one who fixed up Norty when he was sick."

"Sick? I heard he was dead."

Kennerly kept grinning. "Well, well. Maybe. But we're growed-up men, ain't we?"

"But you believe in demons."

Kennerly looked affronted. "That's a lot different."

The gunslinger took off his hat and wiped his forehead. The sun was hot, beating steadily. Kennerly seemed not to notice. In the thin shadow by the livery, the baby girl was gravely smearing dirt on her face.

"You don't know what's after the desert?"

Kennerly shrugged. "Some might. The coach ran through part of it fifty years ago. My pap said so. He used to say 'twas mountains. Others say an ocean . . . a green ocean with monsters. And some say that's where the world ends. That there ain't nothing but lights that'll drive a man blind and the face of God with his mouth open to eat them up."

"Drivel," the gunslinger said shortly.

"Sure it is." Kennerly cried happily. He cringed again, hating, fearing, wanting to please.

"You see my mule is looked after." He flicked Kennerly

another coin, which Kennerly caught on the fly.

"Surely. You stayin' a little?"

"I guess I might."

"That Allie's pretty nice when she wants to be, ain't she?"

"Did you say something?" The gunslinger asked remotely.

Sudden terror dawned in Kennerly's eyes, like twin moons coming over the horizon. "No, sir, not a word. And I'm sorry if I did." He caught sight of Soobie leaning out a window and whirled on her. "I'll whale you now, you little slut-face! 'Fore God! I'll — "

The gunslinger walked away, aware that Kennerly had turned to watch him, aware of the fact that he could whirl and catch the hostler with some true and untinctured emotion distilled on his face. He let it slip. It was hot. The only sure thing about the desert was its size. And it wasn't all played out in this town. Not yet.

XI

They were in bed when Sheb kicked the door open and came in with the knife.

It had been four days, and they had gone by in a blinking haze. He ate. He slept. He made sex with Allie. He found that she played the fiddle and he made her play it for him. She sat by the window in the milky light of daybreak, only a profile, and played something haltingly that might have been good if she had been trained. He felt a growing (but strangely absent-minded) affection for her and thought this might be the trap the man in black had left behind. He read dry and tattered back issues of magazines with faded pictures. He thought very little about everything.

He didn't hear the little piano player come up — his

reflexes had sunk. That didn't seem to matter either, although it would have frightened him badly in another time and place.

Allie was naked, the sheet below her breasts, and they were preparing to make love.

"Please," she was saying. "Like before, I want that, I want — "

The door crashed open and the piano player made his ridiculous, knock-kneed run for the sun. Allie did not scream, although Sheb held an eight-inch carving knife in his hand. Sheb was making a noise, an inarticulate blabbering. He sounded like a man being drowned in a bucket of mud. Spittle flew. He brought the knife down with both hands, and the gunslinger caught his wrists and turned them. The knife went flying. Sheb made a high screeching noise, like a rusty screen door. His hands fluttered in marionette movements, both wrists broken. The wind gritted against the window. Allie's glass on the wall, faintly clouded and distorted, reflected the room.

"She was mine!" He wept. "She was mine first! Mine!"

Allie looked at him and got out of bed. She put on a wrapper, and the gunslinger felt a moment of empathy for a man who must be seeing himself coming out on the far end of what he once had. He was just a little man, and gelded.

"It was for you," Sheb sobbed. "It was only for you, Allie. It was you first and it was all for you. I — ah, oh God, dear God — " The words dissolved into a paroxysm of unintelligibilities, finally to tears. He rocked back and forth, holding his broken wrists to his belly.

"Shhh. Shhh. Let me see." She knelt beside him. "Broken. Sheb, you ass. Didn't you know you were never strong?" She helped him to his feet. He tried to hold his hands to his face, but they would not obey, and he wept nakedly. "Come on over to the table and let me see what I can do."

She led him to the table and set his wrists with slats of

kindling from the fire box. He wept weakly and without volition, and left without looking back.

She came back to the bed. "Where were we?"

"No," he said.

She said patiently, "You knew about that. There's nothing to be done. What else is there?" She touched his shoulder. "Except I'm glad that you are so strong."

"Not now," he said thickly.

"I can make you strong — "

"No," he said. "You can't do that."

XII

The next night the bar was closed. It was whatever passed for the Sabbath in Tull. The gunslinger went to the tiny, leaning church by the graveyard while Allie washed tables with strong disinfectant and rinsed kerosene lamp chimnies in soapy water.

An odd purple dusk had fallen, and the church, lit from the inside, looked almost like a blast furnace from the road.

"I don't go," Allie had said shortly. "The woman who preaches has poison religion. Let the respectable ones go."

He stood in the vestibule, hidden in a shadow, looking in. The pews were gone and the congregation stood (he saw Kennerly and his brood; Castner, owner of the town's scrawny dry-goods emporium and his slat-sided wife; a few barflies; a few "town" women he had never seen before; and, surprisingly, Sheb). They were singing a hymn raggedly, *a cappella*. He looked curiously at the mountainous woman at the pulpit. Allie had said: "She lives alone, hardly ever sees anybody. Only comes out on Sunday to serve up the hellfire. Her name is Sylvia Pittston. She's crazy, but she's got the hoodoo on them. They like it that way. It suits them."

No description could take the measure of the woman.

Breasts like earthworks. A huge pillar of a neck overtopped by a pasty white moon of a face, in which blinked eyes so large and so dark that they seemed to be bottomless tarns. Her hair was a beautiful rich brown and it was piled atop her head in a haphazard, lunatic sprawl, held by a hairpin big enough to be a meat skewer. She wore a dress that seemed to be made of burlap. The arms that held the hymnal were slabs. Her skin was creamy, unmarked, lovely. He thought that she must top three hundred pounds. He felt a sudden red lust for her that made him feel shaky, and he turned his head and looked away.

"Shall we gather at the river,
The beautiful, the beautiful,
The riiiiver,
Shall we gather at the river,
That flows by the Kingdom of God."

The last note of the last chorus faded off, and there was a moment of shuffling and coughing.

She waited. When they were settled, she spread her hands over them, as if in benediction. It was an evocative gesture.

"My dear little brothers and sisters in Christ."

It was a haunting line. For a moment the gunslinger felt mixed feelings of nostalgia and fear, stitched in with an eerie feeling of *deja vu* — he thought: I dreamed this. When? He shook it off. The audience — perhaps twenty-five all told — had become dead silent.

"The subject of our meditation tonight is The Interloper." Her voice was sweet, melodious, the speaking voice of a well-trained soprano.

"A little rustle ran through the audience.

"I feel," Sylvia Pittston said reflectively, "I feel that I know everyone in The Book personally. In the last five years I have worn out five Bibles, and uncountable numbers before that. I love the story, and I love the players in that story. I have walked arm in arm in the lion's den with

Daniel. I stood with David when he was tempted by Bath-sheba as she bathed at the pool. I have been in the fiery furnace with Shadrach, Meshach, and Abednego. I slew two thousand with Samson and was blinded with St. Paul on the road to Damascus. I wept with Mary at Golgotha."

A soft, shurring sigh in the audience.

"I have known and loved them. There is only one — *one* — " she held up a finger — "only one player in the greatest of all dramas that I do not know. Only *one* who stands outside with his face in the shadow. Only *one* that makes my body tremble and my spirit quail. I fear him. I don't know his mind and I fear him. I fear The Interloper."

Another sigh. One of the women had put a hand over her mouth as if to stop a sound and was rocking, rocking.

"The Interloper who came to Eve as a snake on its belly, grinning and writhing. The Interloper who walked among the Children of Israel while Moses was up on the Mount, who whispered to them to make a golden idol, a golden calf, and to worship it with foulness and fornication."

Moans, nods.

"The Interloper! He stood on the balcony with Jezebel and watched as King Ahaz fell screaming to his death, and he and she grinned as the dogs gathered and lapped up his life's blood. Oh, my little brothers and sisters, watch thou for The Interloper."

"Yes, O Jesus — " The man the gunslinger had first noticed coming into town, the one with the straw hat.

"He's always been there, my brothers and sisters. But I don't know his mind. And you don't know his mind. Who could understand the awful darkness that swirls there, the pride like pylons, the titanic blasphemy, the unholy glee? And the madness! The cyclopean, gibbering madness that walks and crawls and wriggles through men's most awful wants and desires?"

"O Jesus Savior — "

"It was *him* who took our Lord up on the mountain — "

"Yes — "

"It was *him* that tempted him and shewed him all the world and the world's pleasures — "

"*Yesss* — "

"It's *him* that will come back when Last Times come on the world . . . and they are coming, my brothers and sisters, can't you feel they are?"

"*Yesss* — "

Rocking and sobbing, the congregation became a sea; the woman seemed to point at all of them, none of them.

"It's *him* that will come as the Antichrist, to lead men into the flaming bowels of perdition, to the bloody end of wickedness, as Star Wormword hangs blazing in the sky, as gall gnaws at the vitals of the children, as women's wombs give forth monstrosities, as the works of men's hands turn to blood — "

"Ahhh — "

"Ah, God — "

"Gawwwwwwww — "

A woman fell on the floor, her legs crashing up and down against the wood. One of her shoes flew off. ·

"It's *him* that stands behind every fleshly pleasure . . . *him!* The Interloper!"

"Yes, Lord!"

A man fell on his knees, holding his head and braying.

"When you take a drink, who holds the bottle?"

"*The Interloper!*"

"When you sit down to a faro or a Watch Me table, who turns the cards?"

"*The Interloper!*"

"When you riot in the flesh of another's body, when you pollute yourself, who are you selling your soul to?"

"*In — *"

"*The —* "

"Oh, Jesus . . . Oh — "

" *— loper —* "

" *— Aw . . . Aw . . . Aw . . .* "

"And who is he?" She screamed (but calm within, he could sense the calmness, the mastery, the control, the domination. He thought suddenly, with terror and absolute surety: he has left a demon in her. She is haunted. He felt the hot ripple of sexual desire again through his fear.)

The man who was holding his head crashed and blundered forward.

"I'm in hell!" He screamed up at her. His face twisted and writhed as if snakes crawled beneath his skin. "I done fornications! I done gambling! I done weed! I done *sins!* I — " But his voice rose skyward in a dreadful, hysterical wail that drowned articulation. He held his head as if it would burst like an overripe cantaloupe at any moment.

The audience stilled as if a cue had been given, frozen in their half-erotic poses of ecstasy.

Sylvia Pittston reached down and grasped his head. The man's cry ceased as her fingers, strong and white, unblemished and gentle, worked through his hair. He looked up at her dumbly.

"Who was with you in sin?" She asked. Her eyes looked into his, deep enough, gentle enough, cold enough to drown in.

"The . . . the Interloper."

"Called who?"

"Called Satan." Raw, oozing whisper.

"Will you renounce?"

Eagerly: "Yes! Yes! Oh, my Jesus Savior!"

She rocked his head; he stared at her with the blank, shiny eyes of the zealot. "If he walked through that door — " she hammered a finger at the vestibule shadows where the gunslinger stood — "would you renounce him to his face?"

"On my mother's name!"

"Do you believe in the eternal love of Jesus?"

He began to weep. "Your fucking-A I do — "

"He forgives you that, Jonson."

"Praise God," Jonson said, still weeping.

"I know he forgives you just as I know he will cast out the unrepentant from his palaces and into the place of burning darkness."

"Praise God." The congregation drained, spoke it solemnly.

"Just as I know this Interloper, this Satan, this Lord of Flies and Serpents will be cast down and crushed . . . will you crush him if you see him, Jonson?"

"Yes and praise God!" Jonson wept.

"Will you crush him if you see him, brothers and sisters?"

"Yess . . . " Sated.

"If you see him sashaying down Main St. tomorrow?"

"Praise God . . . "

The gunslinger, unsettled, at the same time, faded back out the door and headed for town. The smell of the desert was clear in the air. Almost time to move on. Almost.

XIII

In bed again.

"She won't see you," Allie said. She sounded frightened. "She doesn't see anybody. She only comes out on Sunday evenings to scare the hell out of everybody."

"How long has she been here?"

"Twelve years or so. Let's not talk about her."

"Where did she come from? Which direction?"

"I don't know." Lying.

"Allie?"

"I don't know!"

"Allie?"

"All right! All right! She came from the dwellers! From the desert!"

"I thought so." He relaxed a little. "Where does she live?"

Her voice dropped a notch. "If I tell you, will you make love to me?"

"You know the answer to that."

She sighed. It was an old, yellow sound, like turning pages. "She has a house over the knoll in back of the church. A little shack. It's where the . . . the real minister used to live until he moved out. Is that enough? Are you satisfied?"

"No. Not yet." And he rolled on top of her.

XIV

It was the last day, and he knew it.

The sky was an ugly, bruised purple, weirdly lit from above with the first fingers of dawn. Allie moved about like a wraith, lighting lamps, tending the corn fritters that spluttered in the skillet. He had loved her hard after she had told him what he had to know, and she had sensed the coming end and had given more than she had ever given, and she had given it with desperation against the coming of dawn, given it with the tireless energy of sixteen. But she was pale this morning, on the brink of menopause again.

She served him without a word. He ate rapidly, chewing, swallowing, chasing each bite with hot coffee. Allie went to the batwings and stood staring out at the morning, at the silent battalions of slow-moving clouds.

"It's going to dust up today."

"I'm not surprised."

"Are you ever?" She asked ironically, and turned to watch him get his hat. He clapped it on his head and brushed past her.

"Sometimes," he told her. He only saw her once more alive.

XV

By the time he reached Sylvia Pittston's shack, the wind had died utterly and the whole world seemed to wait. He had been in desert country long enough to know that the longer the lull, the harder the wind would blow when it finally decided to start up. A queer, flat light hung over everything.

There was a large wooden cross nailed to the door of the place, which was leaning and tired. He rapped and waited. No answer. He rapped again. No answer. He drew back and kicked in the door with one hard shot of his right boot. A small bolt on the inside ripped free. The door banged against a haphazardly planked wall and scared rats into skittering flight. Sylvia Pittston sat in the hall, sat in a mammoth darkwood rocker, and looked at him calmly with those great and dark eyes. The stormlight fell on her cheeks in terrifying half-tones. She wore a shawl. The rocker made tiny squeaking noises.

They looked at each other for a long, clockless moment.

"You will never catch him," she said. "You walk in the way of evil."

"He came to you," the gunslinger said.

"And to my bed. He spoke to me in the Tongue. He — "

"He screwed you."

She did not flinch. "You walk an evil way, gunslinger. You stand in shadows. You stood in the shadows of the holy place last night. Did you think I couldn't see you?"

"Why did he heal the weed-eater?"

"He was an angel of God. He said so."

"I hope he smiled when he said it."

She drew her lip back from her teeth in an unconsciously feral gesture. "He told me you would follow. He told me what to do. He said you are the Antichrist."

The gunslinger shook his head. "He didn't say that."

She smiled up at him lazily. "He said you would want to bed me. Do you?"

"Yes."

"The price is your life, gunslinger. He has got me with child . . . the child of an angel. If you invade me — " She let the lazy smile complete her thought. At the same time she gestured with her huge, mountainous thighs. They stretched beneath her garment like pure marble slabs. The effect was dizzying.

The gunslinger dropped his hands to the butts of his pistols. "You have a demon, woman. I can remove it."

The effect was instantaneous. She recoiled against the chair, and a weasel look flashed on her face. "Don't touch me! Don't come near me! You dare not touch the Bride of God!"

"Want to bet?" the gunslinger said, grinning. He stepped toward her.

The flesh on the huge frame quaked. Her face had become a caricature of crazed terror, and she stabbed the sign of the Eye at him with pronged fingers.

"The desert," the gunslinger said. "What after the desert?"

"You'll never catch him! Never! Never! You'll burn! He told me so!"

"I'll catch him," the gunslinger said. "We both know it. What is beyond the desert?"

"No!"

"Answer me!"

"No!"

He slid forward, dropped to his knees, and grabbed her thighs. Her legs locked like a vise. She made strange, lustful keening noises.

"The demon, then," he said.

"No — "

He pried the legs apart and unholstered one of his guns.

"No! No! No!" Her breath came in short, savage grunts.

"Answer me."

She rocked in the chair and the floor trembled. Prayers and garbled bits of jargon flew from her lips.

He rammed the barrel of the gun forward. He could feel the terrified wind sucked into her lungs more than he could hear it. Her hands beat at his head; her legs drummed against the floor. And at the same time the huge body tried to take the invader and enwomb it. Outside nothing watched them but the bruised sky.

She screamed something, high and inarticulate.

"What?"

"Mountains!"

"What about them?"

"He stops . . . on the other side . . . s-s-sweet *Jesus!* . . . to m-make his strength. Med-m-meditation, do you under-stand? Oh . . . I'm . . . I'm . . . "

The whole huge mountain of flesh suddenly strained forward and upward, yet he was careful not to let her secret flesh touch him.

Then she seemed to wilt and grow smaller, and she wept with her hands in her lap.

"So," he said, getting up. "The demon is served, eh?"

"Get out. You've killed the child. Get out. Get out."

He stopped at the door and looked back. "No child," he said briefly. "No angel, no demon."

"Leave me alone."

He did.

XVI

By the time he arrived at Kennerly's, a queer obscurity had come over the northern horizon and he knew it was dust. Over Tull the air was still dead quiet.

Kennerly was waiting for him on the chaff-strewn stage that was the floor of his barn. "Leaving?" He grinned abjectly at the gunslinger.

"Yes."

"Not before the storm?"

"Ahead of it."

"The wind goes faster than a man on a mule. In the open it can kill you."

"I'll want the mule now," the gunslinger said simply.

"Sure." But Kennerly did not turn away, merely stood as if searching for something further to say, grinning his groveling, hate-filled grin, and his eyes flicked up and over the gunslinger's shoulder.

The gunslinger sidestepped and turned at the same time, and the heavy stick of stovewood that the girl Soobie held swished through the air, grazing his elbow only. She lost hold of it with the force of her swing and it clattered over the floor. In the explosive height of the loft, barnswallows took shadowed wing.

The girl looked at him bovinely. Her breasts thrust with overripe grandeur at the wash-faded shirt she wore. One thumb sought the haven of her mouth with dreamlike slowness.

The gunslinger turned back to Kennerly. Kennerly's grin was huge. His skin was waxy yellow. His eyes rolled in their sockets. "I — " he began in a phlegm-filled whisper and could not continue.

"The mule," the gunslinger prodded gently.

"Sure, sure, sure," Kennerly whispered, the grin now touched with incredulity. He shuffled after it.

He moved to where he could watch Kennerly, The

hostler brought the mule back and handed him the bridle. "You get in an' tend your sister," he said to Soobie.

Soobie tossed her head and didn't move.

The gunslinger left them there, staring at each other across the dusty, droppings-strewn floor, he with his sick grin, she with dumb, inanimate defiance. Outside the heat was still like a hammer.

XVII

He walked the mule up the center of the street, his boots sending up squirts of dust. His waterbags were strapped across the mule's back.

He stopped at Sheb's, and Allie was not there. The place was deserted, battened for the storm, but still dirty from the night before. She had not begun her cleaning and the place was as fetid as a wet dog.

He filled his tote sack with corn meal, dried and roasted corn, and half of the raw hamburg in the cooler. He left four gold pieces stacked on the planked counter. Allie did not come down. Sheb's piano bid him a silent, yellow-toothed good-by. He stepped back out and cinched the tote sack across the mule's back. There was a tight feeling in his throat. He might still avoid the trap, but the chances were small. He was, after all, the interloper.

He walked past the shuttered, waiting buildings, feeling the eyes that peered through cracks and chinks. The man in black had played God in Tull. Was it only a sense of the cosmic comic, or a matter of desperation? It was a question of some importance.

There was a shrill, harried scream from behind him, and doors suddenly threw themselves open. Forms lunged. The trap was sprung, then. Men in longhandles and men in dirty dungarees. Women in slacks and in faded dresses.

Even children, tagging after their parents. And in every hand there was a chunk of wood or a knife.

His reaction was automatic, instantaneous, inbred. He whirled on his heels while his hands pulled the guns from their holsters, the hafts heavy and sure in his hands. It was Allie, and of course it had to be Allie, coming at him with her face distorted, the scar a hellish purple in the lowering light. He saw that she was held hostage; the distorted, grimacing face of Sheb peered over her shoulder like a witch's familiar. She was his shield and sacrifice. He saw it all, clear and shadowless in the frozen deathless light of the sterile calm, and heard her:

"He's got me O Jesus don't shoot don't don't *don't* — "

But the hands were trained. He was the last of his breed and it was not only his mouth that knew the High Speech. The guns beat their heavy, atonal music into the air. Her mouth flapped and she sagged and the guns fired again. Sheb's head snapped back. They both fell into the dust.

Sticks flew through the air, rained on him. He staggered, fended them off. One with a nail pounded raggedly through it ripped at his arm and drew blood. A man with a beard stubble and sweat-stained armpits lunged flying at him with a dull kitchen knife held in one paw. The gunslinger shot him dead and the man thumped into the street. His teeth clicked audibly as his chin struck.

"SATAN!" Some was screaming: "THE ACCURSED! BRING HIM DOWN!"

"THE INTERLOPER!" Another voice cried. Sticks rained on him. A knife struck his boot and bounced. "THE INTERLOPER! THE ANTICHRIST!"

He blasted his way through the middle of them, running as the bodies fell, his hands picking the targets with dreadful accuracy. Two men and a woman went down, and he ran through the hole they left.

He led them a feverish parade across the street and toward the rickety general store/barber shop that faced Sheb's. He mounted the boardwalk, turned again, and fired the rest of his loads into the charging crowd. Behind them, Sheb and Allie and the others lay crucified in the dust.

They never hesitated or faltered, although every shot he fired found a vital spot and although they had probably never seen a gun except for pictures in old magazines.

He retreated, moving his body like a dancer to avoid the flying missiles. He reloaded as he went, with a rapidity that had also been trained into his fingers. They shuttled busily between gunbelts and cylinders. The mob came up over the boardwalk and he stepped into the general store and rammed the door closed. The large display window to the right shattered inward and three men crowded through. Their faces were zealously blank, their eyes filled with bland fire. He shot them all, and the two that followed them. They fell in the window, hung on the jutting shards of glass, choking the opening.

The door crashed and shuddered with their weight and he could hear *her* voice: "THE KILLER! YOUR SOULS! THE CLOVEN HOOF!"

The door ripped off its hinges and fell straight in, making a flat handclap. Dust puffed up from the floor. Men, women, and children charged him. Spittle and stove-wood flew. He shot his guns empty and they fell like nine-pins. He retreated, shoving over a flour barrel, rolling it at them, into the barbershop, throwing a pan of boiling water that contained two nicked straight-razors. They came on, screaming with frantic incoherency. From somewhere, Sylvia Pittston exhorted them, her voice rising and falling on blind inflections. He pushed shells into hot chambers, smelling the smells of shave and tonsure, smelling his own flesh as the calluses at the tips of his fingers singed.

He went through the back door and onto the porch. The flat scrubland was at his back now, flatly denying the town that crouched against its huge haunch. Three men hustled around the corner, with large betrayer grins on their faces. They saw him, saw him seeing them, and the grins curdled in the second before he mowed them down. A woman had followed them, howling. She was large and fat and known to the patrons of Sheb's as Aunt Mill. The gunslinger blew her backwards and she landed in a whorish sprawl, her skirt kinked up between her thighs.

He went down the steps and walked backwards into the desert, ten paces, twenty. The back door of the barber shop flew open and they boiled out. He caught a glimpse of Sylvia Pittston. He opened up. They fell in squats, they fell backwards, they tumbled over the railing into the dust. They cast no shadows in the deathless purple light of the day. He realized he was screaming. He had been screaming all along. His eyes felt like cracked ball bearings. His balls had drawn up against his belly. His legs were wood. His ears were iron.

The guns were empty and they boiled at him, transmogrified into an Eye and a Hand, and he stood, screaming and reloading, his mind far away and absent, letting his hands do their reloading trick. Could he hold up a hand, tell them he had spent twenty-five years learning this trick and others, tell them of the guns and the blood that had blessed them? Not with his mouth. But his hands could speak their own tale.

They were in throwing range as he finished reloading, and a stick struck him on the forehead and brought blood in abraded drops. In two seconds they would be in gripping distance. In the forefront he saw Kennerly; Kennerly's younger daughter, perhaps eleven; Soobie; two male barflies; a female barfly named Amy Feldon. He let them all have it, and the ones behind them. Their bodies thumped like scarecrows. Blood and brains flew in streamers.

They halted for a moment, startled, the mob face shivering into individual, bewildered faces. A man ran in a large, screaming circle. A woman with blisters on her hands turned her head up and cackled feverishly at the sky. The man whom he had first seen sitting gravely on the steps of the mercantile store made a sudden and amazing load in his pants.

He had time to reload one gun.

Then it was Sylvia Pittston, running at him, waving a wooden cross in each hand. "DEVIL! DEVIL! DEVIL! CHILD-KILLER! MONSTER! DESTROY HIM, BROTHERS AND SISTERS! DESTROY THE CHILD-KILLING INTERLOPER!"

He put a shot into each of the crosspieces, blowing the roods to splinters, and four more into the woman's head. She seemed to accordian into herself and waver like a shimmer of heat.

They all stared at her for a moment in tableau, while the gunslinger's fingers did their reloading trick. The tips of his fingers sizzled and burned. Neat circles were branded into the tips of each one.

There were less of them, now; he had run through them like a mower's sycthe. He thought they would break with the woman dead, but someone threw a knife. The hilt struck him squarely between the eyes and knocked him over. They ran at him in a reaching, vicious clot. He fired his guns empty again, lying in his own spent shells. His head hurt and he saw large brown circles in front of his eyes. He missed one shot, downed eleven.

But they were on him, the ones that were left. He fired the four shells he had reloaded, and then they were beating him, stabbing him. He threw a pair of them off his left arm and rolled away. His hands began doing their infallible trick. He was stabbed in the shoulder. He was stabbed in the

back. He was hit across the ribs. He was stabbed in the ass.
A small boy squirmed at him and made the only deep cut,
across the bulge of his calf. The gunslinger blew his head
off.

They were scattering and he let them have it again. The
ones left began to retreat toward the sand-colored, pitted
buildings, and still the hands did their trick, like over-
eager dogs that want to do their rolling-over trick for you
not once or twice but all night, and the hands were cutting
them down as they ran. The last one made it as far as the
steps of the barber shop's back porch, and then the gunslinger's bullet took him in the back of the head.

Silence came back in, filling jagged spaces.

The gunslinger was bleeding from perhaps twenty
different wounds, all of them shallow except for the cut
across his calf. He bound it with a strip of shirt and then
straightened and examined his kill.

They trailed in a twisted, zigzagging path from the back
door of the barber shop to where he stood. They lay in all
positions. None of them seemed to be sleeping.

He followed them back, counting as he went. In the
general store one man lay with his arms wrapped lovingly
around the cracked candy jar he had dragged down with
him.

He ended up where he had started, in the middle of
the deserted main street. He had shot and killed thirty-nine
men, fourteen women, and five children. He had shot and
killed everyone in Tull.

A sickish-sweet odor came to him on the first of the dry,
stirring wind. He followed it, then looked up and nodded.
The decaying body of Nort was spread-eagled atop the plank
roof of Sheb's, crucified with wooden pegs. Mouth and eyes
were open. A large and purple cloven hoof had been pressed
into the skin of his grimy forehead.

He walked out of town. His mule was standing in a

clump of weed about forty yards out along the remnant of the coach road. The gunslinger led it back to Kennerly's stable. Outside, the wind was playing a jagtime tune. He put the mule up and went back to Sheb's. He found a ladder in the back shed, went up to the roof, and cut Nort down. The body was lighter than a bag of sticks. He tumbled it down to join the common people. Then he went back inside, ate hamburgers and drank three beers while the light failed and the sand began to fly. That night he slept in the bed where he and Allie had lain. He had no dreams. The next morning the wind was gone and the sun was its usual bright and forgetful self. The bodies had gone south like tumble-weeds with the wind. At midmorning, after he had bound all his cuts, he moved on as well.

XVIII

He thought Brown had fallen asleep. The fire was down to a spark and the bird, Zoltan, had put his head under his wing.

Just as he was about to get up and spread a pallet in the corner, Brown said, "There. You've told it. Do you feel better?"

The gunslinger started. "Why would I feel bad?"

"You're human, you said. No demon. Or did you lie?"

"I didn't lie." He felt the grudging admittance in him: he liked Brown. Honestly did. And he hadn't lied to the dweller in any way. "Who are you, Brown? Really, I mean."

"Just me," he said, unperturbed. "Why do you have to think you're such a mystery?"

The gunslinger lit a smoke without replying.

"I think you're very close to your man in black," Brown said. "Is he desperate?"

"I don't know."

"Are you?"

"Not yet," the gunslinger said. He looked at Brown with a shade of defiance. "I do what I have to do."

"That's good then," Brown said and turned over and went to sleep.

XIX

In the morning Brown fed him and sent him on his way. In the daylight he was an amazing figure with his scrawny, burnt chest, pencil-like collarbones and ring-leted shock of red hair. The bird perched on his shoulder.

"The mule?" The gunslinger asked.

"I'll eat it," Brown said.

"Okay."

Brown offered his hand and the gunslinger shook it. The dweller nodded to the south. "Walk easy."

"You know it."

They nodded at each other and then the gunslinger walked away, his body festooned with guns and water. He looked back once. Brown was rooting furiously at his little cornbed. The crow was perched on the low roof of his dwelling like a gargoyle.

XX

The fire was down, and the stars had begun to pale off. The wind walked restlessly. The gunslinger twitched in his sleep and was still again. He dreamed a thirsty dream. In the darkness the shape of the mountains was invisible. The thoughts of guilt had faded. The desert had baked them out. He found himself thinking more and more about Cort, who had taught him to shoot, instead. Cort had known black from white.

He stirred again and awoke. He blinked at the dead fire with its own shape superimposed over the other, more geometrical one. He was a romantic, he knew it, and he guarded the knowledge jealously.

That, of course, made him think of Cort again. He didn't know where Cort was. The world had moved on.

The gunslinger shouldered his tote sack and moved on with it.

THE
WAY STATION

A nursery rhyme had been playing itself through his mind all day, the maddening kind of thing that will not let go, that stands mockingly outside the apse of the conscious mind and makes faces at the rational being inside. The rhyme was:

The rain in Spain falls mainly on the plain.
There is joy and also pain
but the rain in Spain falls mainly on the plain.

Pretty-plain, loony-sane
The ways of the world all will change
and all the ways remain the same
but if you're mad or only sane
the rain in Spain falls mainly on the plain.

We walk in love but fly in chains
And the planes in Spain fall mainly in the rain.

He knew why the rhyme had occurred to him. There had been the recurring dream of his room in the castle and of his father, who had sung it to him as he lay solemnly in the tiny bed by the window of many colors. She did not sing it at bedtimes because all small boys born to the High Speech must face the dark alone, but she sang to him at naptimes and he could remember the heavy gray rainlight that

71

shivered into colors on the counterpane; he could feel the
coolness of the room and the heavy warmth of blankets, love
for his mother and her red lips, the haunting melody of the
little nonsense lyric, and her voice.

Now it came back maddeningly, like prickly heat, chasing its own tail in his mind as he walked. All his water was
gone, and he knew he was very likely a dead man. He had
never expected it to come to this, and he was sorry. Since
noon he had been watching his feet rather than watching
the way ahead. Out here even the devil-grass had grown
stunted and yellow. The hardpan had disintegrated in
places to mere rubble. The mountains were not noticeably
clearer, although sixteen days had passed since he had left
the hut of the last homesteader, a loony-sane young man on
the edge of the desert. He had had a raven, the gunslinger
remembered, but he couldn't remember the raven's name.

He watched his feet move up and down, listened to the
nonsense rhyme sing itself into a pitiful garble in his mind,
and wondered when he would fall down for the first time.
He didn't want to fall, even though there was no one to see
him. It was a matter of pride. A gunslinger knows pride —
that invisible bone that keeps the neck stiff.

He stopped and looked up suddenly. It made his head
buzz and for a moment his whole body seemed to float. The
mountains dreamed against the far horizon. But there was
something else up ahead, something much closer. Perhaps
only five miles away. He squinted at it, but his eyes were
sandblasted and going glareblind. He shook his head and
began to walk again. The rhyme circled and buzzed. About
an hour later he fell down and skinned his hands. He looked
at the tiny beads of blood on his flaked skin with unbelief.
The blood looked no thinner; it looked mutely viable. It
seemed almost as smug as the desert. He dashed the drops
away, hating them blindly. Smug? Why not? The blood was

not thirsty. The blood was being served. The blood was being made sacrifice unto. Blood sacrifice. All the blood needed to do was run . . . and run . . . and run.

He looked at the splotches that had landed on the hard-pan and watched as they were sucked up with uncanny suddenness. How do you like that, blood? How does that grab you?

O Jesus, you're far gone.

He got up, holding his hands to his chest and the thing he had seen earlier was almost in front of him, startling a cry out of him — a dust-choked crow-croak. It was a building. No; two buildings, surrounded by a fallen rail fence. The wood seemed old, fragile to the point of elvishness; it was wood being transmogrified into sand. One of the buildings had been a stable — the shape was clear and unmistakable. The other was a house, or an inn. A way station for the coach line. The tottering sand-house (the wind had crusted the wood with grit until it looked like a sand castle that the sun had beat upon at low tide and hardened to a temporary abode) cast a thin line of shadow, and someone sat in the shadow, leaning against the building. And the building seemed to lean with the burden of his weight.

Him, then. At last. The man in black.

The gunslinger stood with his hands to his chest, unaware of his declamatory posture, and gawped. And instead of the tremendous winging excitement he had expected (or perhaps fear, or awe), there was nothing but the dim, atavistic guilt for the sudden, raging hate of his own blood moments earlier and the endless ring-a-rosy of the childhood song:

. . . *the rain in Spain* . . .

He moved forward, drawing one gun.

. . . *falls mainly on the plain.*

He came the last quarter mile at the run, not trying to

hide himself; there was nothing to hide behind. His short shadow raced him. He was not aware that his face had become a gray and grinning deathmask of exhaustion; he was aware of nothing but the figure in the shadow. It did not occur to him until later that the figure might even have been dead.

He kicked through one of the leaning fence rails (it broke in two without a sound, almost apologetically) and lunged across the dazzled and silent stable yard, bringing the gun up.

"You're covered! You're covered! You're — "

The figure moved restlessly and stood up. The gunslinger thought: My God, he is worn away to nothing, what's happened to him? Because the man in black had shrunk two full feet and his hair had gone white.

He paused, struck dumb, his head buzzing tunelessly. His heart was racing at a lunatic rate and he thought, I'm dying right here —

He sucked the white-hot air into his lungs and hung his head for a moment. When he raised it again, he saw it wasn't the man in black but a small boy with sun-bleached hair, regarding him with eyes that did not even seem interested. The gunslinger stared at him blankly and then shook his head in negation. But the boy survived his refusal to believe; he was still there, wearing blue jeans with a patch on one knee and a plain brown shirt of rough weave.

The gunslinger shook his head again and started for the stable with his head lowered, gun still in hand. He couldn't think yet. His head was filled with motes and there was a huge, thrumming ache building in it.

The inside of the stable was silent and dark and exploding with heat. The gunslinger stared around himself with huge, floating walleyes. He made a drunken about-face and saw the boy standing in the ruined doorway, staring at him. A huge lancet of pain slipped dreamily into his head, cutting from temple to temple, dividing his brain like an orange. He reholstered his gun, swayed, put out his hands as if to ward off phantoms, and fell over on his face.

When he woke up, he was on his back, and there was a pile of light, odorless hay beneath his head. The boy had not been able to move him, but he had made him reasonably comfortable. And he was cool. He looked down at himself and saw that his shirt was dark with moisture. He licked at his face and tasted water. He blinked at it.

The boy was hunkered down beside him. When he saw the gunslinger's eyes were open, he reached behind him and gave the gunslinger a dented tin can filled with water. He grasped it with trembling hands and allowed himself to drink a little — just a little. When that was down and sitting in his belly, he drank a little more. Then he spilled the rest over his face and made shocked blowing noises. The boy's pretty lips curved in a solemn little smile.

"Want something to eat?"

"Not yet," the gunslinger said. There was still a sick ache in his head from the sunstroke, and the water sat uneasily in his stomach, as if it did not know where to go. "Who are you?"

"My name is John Chambers. You can call me Jake."

The gunslinger sat up, and the sick ache became hard and immediate. He leaned forward and lost a brief struggle with his stomach.

"There's more," Jake said. He took the can and walked toward the rear of the stable. He paused and smiled back at the gunslinger uncertainly. The gunslinger nodded at him and then put his head down and propped it with his hands. The boy was well-made, handsome, perhaps nine. There had been a shadow on his face, but there were shadows on all faces now.

A strange, thumping hum began at the rear of the stable, and the gunslinger raised his head alertly, hands going to gunbutts. The sound lasted for perhaps fifteen seconds and then quit. The boy came back with the can — filled now.

The gunslinger drank sparingly again, and this time it was a little better. The ache in his head was fading.

"I didn't know what to do with you when you fell down," Jake said. "For a couple of seconds there, I thought you were going to shoot me."

"I thought you were somebody else."

"The priest?"

The gunslinger looked up sharply. "What priest?"

The boy looked at him, frowning lightly. "The priest. He camped in the yard. I was in the house over there. I didn't like him, so I didn't come out. He came in the night and went on the next day. I would have hidden from you, but I was sleepin' when you came." He looked darkly over the gunslinger's head. "I don't like people. They fuck me up."

"What did the priest look like?"

The boy shrugged. "Like a priest. He was wearing black things."

"Like a hood and a cassock?"

"What's a cassock?"

"A robe."

The boy nodded. "A robe and a hood."

The gunslinger leaned forward, and something in his face made the boy recoil a little. "How long ago?"

"I — I — "

Patiently, the gunslinger said, "I'm not going to hurt you."

"I don't know. I can't remember time. Every day is the same."

For the first time the gunslinger wondered consciously how the boy had come to this place, with dry and man-killing leagues of desert all around it. But he would not make it his concern; not yet, at least. "Make a guess. Long ago?"

"No. Not long. I haven't been here long."

The fire lit in him again. He grabbed the can and drank from it with hands that trembled the smallest bit. A snatch of the cradle song recurred, but this time, instead of his mother's face, he saw the scarred face of Alice, who had been his woman in the now-defunct town of Tull. "How long? A week? Two? three?"

The boy looked at him distractedly. "Yes."

"Which one?"

"A week. Or two. I didn't come out. He didn't even drink. I thought he might be the ghost of a priest. I was scared. I've been scared almost all the time." His face quivered like crystal on the edge of the ultimate, destructive high note. "He didn't even build a fire. He just sat there. I don't even know if he went to sleep."

Close! He was closer than he had ever been. In spite of his extreme dehydration, his hands felt faintly moist; greasy.

"There's some dried meat," the boy said.

"All right." The gunslinger nodded. "Good."

The boy got up to fetch it, his knees popping slightly. He made a fine straight figure. The desert had not yet sapped him. His arms were thin, but the skin, although tanned, had not dried and cracked. He's got juice, the gunslinger thought. He drank from the can again. He's got juice and he didn't come from this place.

Jake came back with a pile of dried jerky on what looked like a sun-scoured breadboard. The meat was tough, stringy, and salty enough to make the cankered lining of the gunslinger's mouth sing. He ate and drank until he felt logy, and then settled back. The boy ate only a little.

The gunslinger regarded him steadily, and the boy looked back at him. "Where did you come from, Jake?" He asked finally.

"I don't know." The boy frowned. "I did know. I knew when I came here, but it's all fuzzy now, like a bad dream when you wake up. I have lots of bad dreams."

"Did somebody bring you?"

"No," the boy said. "I was just here."

"You're not making any sense," the gunslinger said flatly.

Quite suddenly the boy seemed on the verge of tears. "I can't help it. I was just here. And now you'll go away and I'll starve because you ate up almost all my food. I didn't ask to be here. I don't like it. It's spooky."

"Don't feel so sorry for yourself. Make do."

"I didn't ask to be here," the boy repeated bewildered defiance.

The gunslinger ate another piece of the meat, chewing the salt out of it before swallowing. The boy had become part of it, and the gunslinger was convinced he told the truth — he had not asked for it. It was too bad. He himself . . . *he* had asked for it. But he had not asked for the game to become this dirty. He had not asked to be allowed to turn his guns on the unarmed populace of Tull; had not asked to shoot Allie, her face marked by that strange, shining scar; had not asked to be faced with a choice between the obsession of his duty and his quest and criminal amorality. The man in black had begun to pull bad strings in his desperation, if it was the man in black who had pulled this particular string. It was not fair to ring in innocent bystanders and make them speak lines they didn't understand on a strange stage. Allie, he thought, Allie at least had been into the world in her own self-illusory way. But this *boy* . . . this God-damned *boy*. . . .

"Tell me what you can remember," he told Jake.

"It's only a little. It doesn't seem to make any sense anymore."

"Tell me. Maybe I can pick up the sense."

"There was a place . . . the one before this one. A high place with lots of rooms and a patio where you could look at tall buildings and water. There was a statue that stood in the water."

"A statue in the water?"

"Yes. A lady with a crown and a torch."

"Are you making this up?"

"I guess I must be," the boy said hopelessly. "There were things to ride in on the streets. Big ones and little ones. Yellow ones. A lot of yellow ones. I walked to school. There were cement paths beside the streets. Windows to look in and more statues wearing clothes. The statues sold the clothes. I know it sounds crazy, but the statues sold the clothes."

The gunslinger shook his head and looked for a lie on the boy's face. He saw none.

"I walked to school," the boy repeated fixedly. "And I had a — " His eyes tilted closed and his lips moved gropingly. " — a brown . . . book . . . bag. I carried a lunch. And I wore — " the groping again, agonized groping " — a tie."

"A what?"

"I don't know." The boy's fingers made a slow, unconscious clinching motion at his throat — a gesture the gunslinger associated with hanging. "I don't know. It's just all gone." And he looked away.

"May I put you to sleep?" The gunslinger asked.

"I'm not sleepy."

"I can make you sleepy, and I can make you remember."

Doubtfully, Jake asked, "How could you do that?"

"With this."

The gunslinger removed one of the shells from his gunbelt and twirled it in his fingers. The movement was dexterous, as flowing as oil. The shell cartwheeled effortlessly from thumb and index and index and second, to second and ring, to ring and pinky. It popped out of sight and reappeared; seemed to float briefly, and then reversed. The shell walked across the gunslinger's fingers. The fingers themselves moved like a beaded curtain in a breeze. The boy watched, his initial doubt replaced with plain delight, then by raptness, then by a dawning mute blankness. The eyes slipped shut. The shell danced back and forth. Jake's eyes opened again, caught the steady, limpid dance between the gunslinger's fingers for a while longer, and then his eyes closed once more. The gunslinger continued, but Jake's eyes did not open again. The boy breathed with steady, bovine calmness. Was this part of it? Yes. There was a certain beauty, a logic, like the lacy frettings that fringe hard blue ice-packs. He seemed to hear the sound of wind-chimes. Not for the first time the gunslinger tasted the smooth, loden taste of soul-sickness. The shell in his fingers, manipulated with such unknown grace, was suddenly undead, horrific, the spoor of a monster. He dropped it into his palm and closed it into a fist with painful force. There were such things as rape in the world. Rape and murder and unspeakable practices, and all of them were for the good, the bloody good, for the myth, for the grail, for the Tower. Ah, the Tower stood somewhere, rearing its black bulk to

the sky, and in his desert-scoured ears, the gunslinger heard the faint sweet sound of wind-chimes.

"Where are you?" he asked.

Jake Chambers is going downstairs with his bookbag. There is Earth Science, there is Economic Geography, there is a notepad, a pencil, a lunch his mother's cook, Mrs. Greta Shaw, has made for him in the chrome-and-formica kitchen where a fan whirrs eternally, sucking up alien odors. In his lunch sack he has a pea-nut butter and jelly sandwich, a balogna, lettuce, and onion sand-wich, and four Oreo cookies. His parents do not hate him, but they seem to have overlooked him. They have abdicated and left him to Mrs. Greta Shaw, to nannies, to a tutor in the summer and The School (which is Private and Nice, and most of all, White) the rest of the time. None of these people have ever pretended to be more than what they are — professional people, the best in their fields. None have folded him to a particularly warm bosom as usually happens in the historical novels his mother reads and which Jake has dipped into, looking for the "hot parts." Hysterical novels, his father sometimes calls them, and sometimes, "bodice-rippers." You should talk, his mother says with infinite scorn from behind some closed door where Jake listens. His father works for The Network, and Jake could pick him out of a line-up. Probably.

Jake does not know that he hates all the professional people, but he does. People have always bewildered him. He likes stairs and will not use the self-service elevator in his building. His mother, who is scrawny in a sexy way, often goes to bed with sick friends.

Now he is on the street, Jake Chambers is on the street, he has "Hit the bricks." He is clean and well-mannered, comely, sensitive. He has no friends; only acquaintances. He has never bothered to think about this, but it hurts him. He does not know or understand that a long association with professional people has caused him to take many of their traits. Mrs. Greta Shaw makes very professional sandwiches. She quarters them and cuts off the breadcrusts so that when he eats in the gym period four he looks like he ought to be at a cocktail party with a drink in his other hand instead of a sports novel from the school library. His father makes a great deal of money because he is a master of "the kill" — that is, placing a stronger show on his Network against a weaker show on a rival Network. His father smokes four packs of cigarettes a day. His father does not cough, but he has a hard grin, like the steak knives they sell in supermarkets.

Down the street. His mother leaves cab fare, but he walks every day it doesn't rain, swinging his bookbag, a small boy who looks very American with his blonde hair and blue eyes. Girls have already begun to notice him (with their mother's approval), and he does not shy away with skittish little-boy arrogance. He talks to them with unknowing professionalism and puzzles them away. He likes geography and bowls in the afternoon. His father owns stock in a company that makes automatic pin-setting machinery, but the bowling alley Jake patronizes does not use his father's brand. He does not think he has thought about this, but he has.

Walking down the street, he passes Brendio's where the models stand dressed in fur coats, in six-button Edwardian suits, some in nothing at all; some are "barenaked." These models — these mannequins — are perfectly professional, and he hates all professionalism. He is too young to have learned to hate himself yet, but that seed is already there; it has been planted in the bitter cleft of his heart.

He comes to the corner and stands with his bookbag at his side. Traffic roars by — grunting busses, taxis, Volkswagens, a large truck. He is just a boy, but not average, and he sees the man who kills him out of the corner of his eye. It is the man in black, and he doesn't see the face, only the swirling robe, the outstretched hands. He falls into the street with his arms outstretched, not letting go of the bookbag which contains Mrs. Greta Shaw's extremely professional lunch. There is a brief glance through a po-

*larized windshield at the horrified face of a businessman wearing
a dark-blue hat in the band of which is a small, jaunty feather. An
old woman on the far curb screams — she is wearing a black hat
with a net. Nothing jaunty about that black net; it is like a mourner's
veil. Jake feels nothing but surprise and his usual sense of headlong bewilderment — is this how it ends? He lands hard in the
street and looks at an asphalt-sealed crack some two inches from
his eyes. The bookbag is jolted from his hand. He is wondering
if he has skinned his knees when the car of the businessman wearing the blue hat with the jaunty feather passes over him. It is a
big blue 1976 Cadillac with sixteen-inch wheels. It is almost exactly the same color as the businessman's hat. It breaks Jake's back,
mushes his stomach, and sends blood from his mouth in a high-
pressure jet. He turns his head and sees the Cadillac's flaming
taillights and smoke spurting from beneath its locked rear wheels.
The car has also run over his bookbag and left a wide black tread
on it. He turns his head the other way and sees a large yellow
Ford screaming to a stop inches from his body. A black fellow
who has been selling pretzels and sodas from a pushcart is coming
toward him on the run. Blood runs from Jake's nose, ears, eyes,
rectum. His genitals have been squashed. He wonders irritably
how badly he has skinned his knees. Now the driver of the Cadillac is running toward him, babbling. Somewhere a terrible, calm
voice, the voice of doom, says: "I am a priest. Let me through. An
act of Contrition — "*

    *He sees the black robe and knows sudden horror. It is him,
the man in black. He turns his face away with the last of his
strength. Somewhere a radio is playing a song by the rock group
Kiss. He sees his own hand trailing on the pavement, small, white,
shapely. He has never bitten his nails.*

    Looking at his hand, Jake dies.

The gunslinger sat in frowning thought. He was tired
and his body ached and the thoughts came with aggravating
slowness. Across from him the amazing boy slept with his

hands folded in his lap, still breathing calmly. He had told his tale without much emotion, although his voice had trembled near the end, when he had come to the part about the "priest" and the "Act of Contrition." He had not, of course, told the gunslinger about his family and his own sense of bewildered dichotomy, but that had seeped through anyway — enough had seeped through to make out its shape. The fact that there had never been such a city as the boy described (or, if so, it had only existed in the myth of prehistory) was not the most upsetting part of the story, but it was disturbing. It was all disturbing. The gunslinger was afraid of the implications.

"Jake?"

"Uh-huh?"

"Do you want to remember this when you wake up, or forget it?"

"Forget it," the boy said promptly. "I bled."

"All right. You're going to sleep, understand? Go ahead and lie over."

Jake laid over, looking small and peaceful and harmless. The gunslinger did not believe he was harmless. There was a deadly feeling about him, and the stink of predestination. He didn't like the feeling, but he liked the boy. He liked him a great deal.

"Jake?"

"Shhh. I want to sleep."

"Yes. And when you wake up you won't remember any of this."

"Kay."

The gunslinger watched him for a brief time, thinking of his own boyhood, which usually seemed to have happened to another person — to a person who had jumped through some osmotic lens and become someone else — but which now seemed poignantly close. It was very hot in the stable of the way station, and he carefully drank some more water. He got up and walked to the back of the building, pausing to look into one of the horse stalls. There was a small pile of white hay in the corner, and a neatly folded blanket, but there was no smell of horse. There was no smell of anything in the stable. The sun had bled away every smell and left nothing. The air was perfectly neutral.

At the back of the stable was a small, dark room with a stainless steel machine in the center. It was untouched by rust or rot. It looked like a butter churn. At the left, a chrome pipe jutted from it, terminating over a drain in the floor. The gunslinger had seen pumps like it in other dry places, but never one so big. He could not contemplate how deep they must have drilled before they struck water, secret and forever black under the desert.

Why hadn't they removed the pump when the way station had been abandoned?

Demons, perhaps.

He shuddered abruptly, an abrupt twisting of his back. Heatflesh poked out on his skin, then receded. He went to the control switch and pushed the ON button. The machine began to hum. After perhaps half a minute, a stream of cool, clear water belched from the pipe and went down the drain to be recirculated. Perhaps three gallons flowed out of the pipe before the pump shut itself down with a final click. It was a thing as alien to this place and time as true love, and yet as concrete as a Judgment, a silent reminder of the time when the world had not yet moved on. It probably ran on an atomic slug, as there was no electricity within a thousand miles of here and even dry batteries would have lost their charge long ago. The gunslinger didn't like it.

He went back and sat down beside the boy, who had put one hand under his cheek. Nice-looking boy. The gunslinger drank some more water and crossed his legs so he was sitting Indian fashion. The boy, like the squatter on the edge of the desert who kept the bird (Zoltan, the gunslinger remembered abruptly, the bird's name was Zoltan), had lost his sense of time, but the fact that the man in black was closer seemed beyond doubt. Not for the first time, the gunslinger wondered if the man in black was letting him catch up for some reason of his own. Perhaps the gunslinger was playing into his hands. He tried to imagine what the confrontation might be like, and could not.

He was very hot, but he no longer felt sick. The nursery rhyme occurred to him again, but this time instead of his mother, he thought of Cort — Cort, with his face hemstitched with the scars of bricks and bullets and blunt instruments. The scars of war. He wondered if Cort had ever had a love to match those monumental scars. He doubted it. He thought of Aileen, and of Marten, that incomplete enchanter.

The gunslinger was not a man to dwell on the past; only a shadowy conception of the future and of his own emotional make-up saved him from being a creature without imagination, a dullard. His present run of thought therefore rather amazed him. Each name called up others — Cuthbert, Paul, the old man Jonas; and Susan, the lovely girl at the window.

The piano player in Tull (also dead, all dead in Tull, and by his hand) had been fond of the old songs, and the gunslinger hummed one tunelessly under his breath:

Love o love o careless love
See what careless love has done.

The gunslinger laughed, bemused. *I am the last of that green and warm-hued world.* And for all his nostalgia, he felt no self-pity. The world had moved on mercilessly, but his legs were still strong, and the man in black was closer. The gunslinger nodded out.

When he woke up it was almost dark and the boy was gone.

The gunslinger got up, hearing his joints pop, and went

to the stable door. There was a small flame dancing in darkness on the porch of the inn. He walked toward it, his shadow long and black and trailing in the ochre light of the sunset.

Jake was sitting by a kerosene lamp. "The oil was in a drum," he said, "but I was scared to burn it in the house. Everything's so dry — "

"You did just right." The gunslinger sat down, seeing but not thinking about the dust of years that puffed up around his rump. The flame from the lamp shadowed the boy's face with delicate tones. The gunslinger produced his poke and rolled a cigarette.

"We have to talk," he said.

Jake nodded.

"I guess you know I'm on the prod for that man you saw."

"Are you going to kill him?"

"I don't know. I have to make him tell me something. I may have to make him take me someplace."

"Where?"

"To find a tower," the gunslinger said. He held his cigarette over the chimney of the lamp and drew on it; the smoke drifted away on the rising night breeze. Jake watched it. His face showed neither fear nor curiosity, certainly not enthusiasm.

"So I'm going on tomorrow," the gunslinger said. "You'll have to come with me. How much of that meat is left?"

"Only a handful."

"Corn?"

"A little."

The gunslinger nodded. "Is there a cellar?"

"Yes." Jake looked at him. The pupils of his eyes had grown to a huge, fragile size. "You pull up on a ring in the floor, but I didn't go down. I was afraid the ladder would break and I wouldn't be able to get up again. And it smells bad. It's the only thing around here that smells at all."

"We'll get up early and see if there's anything down there worth taking. Then we'll bug out."

"All right." The boy paused and then said, "I'm glad I didn't kill you when you were sleeping. I had a pitchfork and I thought about doing it. But I didn't, and now I won't have to be afraid to go to sleep."

"What would you be afraid of?"

The book looked at him ominously. "Spooks. Of *him* coming back."

"The man in black," the gunslinger said. Not a question.

"Yes. Is he a bad man?"

"That depends on where you're standing," the gunslinger said absently. He got up and pitched his cigarette out onto the hardpan. "I'm going to sleep."

The boy looked at him timidly. "Can I sleep in the stable with you?"

"Of course."

The gunslinger stood on the steps, looking up, and the boy joined him. Polaris was up there, and Mars. It seemed to the gunslinger that, if he closed his eyes he would be able to hear the croaking of the first spring peepers, smell the green and almost-summer smell of the court lawns after their first cutting (and hear, perhaps, the indolent click of croquet balls as the ladies of the East Wing, attired only in their shifts as dusk glimmered toward dark, played at Points), could almost see Aileen as she came through the break in the hedges —

It was not like him to think so much of the past.

He turned back and picked up the lamp. "Let's go to sleep," he said.

They crossed to the stable together.

The next morning he explored the cellar.

Jake was right; it smelled bad. It had a wet, swampy smell that made the gunslinger feel nauseous and a little lightheaded after the antiseptic odorlessness of the desert and the stable. The cellar smelled of cabbages and turnips and potatoes with long, sightless eyes gone to everlasting rot. The ladder, however, seemed quite sturdy, and he climbed down.

The floor was earthen, and his head almost touched the overhead beams. Down here spiders still lived, disturbingly big ones with mottled gray bodies. Many of them had mutated. Some had eyes on stalks, some had what might have been as many as sixteen legs.

The gunslinger peered around and waited for his nighteyes.

"You all right?" Jake called down nervously.

"Yes. He focused on the corner. "There are cans. Wait."

He went carefully to the corner, ducking his head. There was an old box with one side folded down. The cans were vegetables — green beans, yellow beans . . . and three cans of corned beef.

He scooped up an armload and went back to the ladder. He climbed halfway up and handed them to Jake, who knelt to receive them. He went back for more.

It was on the third trip that he heard the groaning in the foundations.

He turned, looked, and felt a kind of dreamy terror wash over him, a feeling both languid and repellent, like sex in the water — one drowning within another.

The foundation was composed of huge sandstone blocks that had probably been evenly cornered when the way station was new, but which were now at every zigzag, drunken angle. It made the wall look as if it were inscribed with strange, meandering hierogliphics. And from the joining of two of these abtruse cracks, a thin spill of sand was running, as if something on the other side was digging itself through with slobbering, agonized intensity.

The groaning rose and fell, becoming louder, until the whole cellar was full of the sound, an abstract noise of ripping pain and dreadful effort.

"Come up!" Jake screamed. "O Jesus, mister, come up!"

"Go away," the gunslinger said calmly.

"Come up!" Jake screamed again.

The gunslinger did not answer. He pulled leather with his right hand.

There was a hole in the wall now, a hole as big as a coin. He could hear, through the curtain of his own terror, Jake's pattering feet as the boy ran. Then the spill of sand stopped. The groaning ceased, but there was a sound of steady, labored breathing.

"Who are you?" The gunslinger asked.

No answer.

And in the High Speech, his voice filling with the old thunder of command, Roland demanded: "Who are you, Demon? Speak, if you would speak. My time is short; my hands lose patience."

"Go slow," a dragging, clotted voice said from within the wall. And the gunslinger felt the dreamlike terror deepen and grow almost solid. It was the voice of Alice, the woman he had stayed with in the town of Tull. But she was dead; he had seen her go down himself, a bullet hole between her eyes. Fathoms seemed to swim by his eyes, descending. "Go slow past the Drawers, gunslinger. While you travel with the boy, the man in black travels with your soul in his pocket."

"What do you mean? Speak on!"

But the breathing was gone.

The gunslinger stood for a moment, frozen, and then one of the huge spiders dropped on his arm and scrambled frantically up to his shoulder. With an involuntary grunt he brushed it away and got his feet moving. He did not want to do it, but custom was strict, inviolable. The dead from the dead, as the old proverb has it; only a corpse may speak. He went to the hole and punched at it. The sandstone crumbled easily at the edges, and with a bare stiffening of muscles, he thrust his hand through the wall.

And touched something solid, with raised and fretted knobs. He drew it out. He held a jawbone, rotted at the far hinge. The teeth leaned this way and that.

"All right," he said softly. He thrust it rudely into his back pocket and went back up the ladder, carrying the last cans awkwardly. He left the trapdoor open. The sun would get in and kill the spiders.

Jake was halfway across the stable yard, cowering on the cracked, rubbly hardpan. He screamed when he saw the gunslinger, backed away a step or two, and then ran to him, crying.

"I thought it got you, that it got you, I thought — "

"It didn't." He held the boy to him, feeling his face, hot against his chest, and his hands, dry against his ribcage. It occurred to him later that this was when he began to love the boy — which was, of course, what the man in black must have planned all along.

"Was it a demon?" The voice was muffled.

"Yes. A speaking-demon. We don't have to go back there anymore. Come on."

They went to the stable, and the gunslinger made a rough pack from the blanket he had slept under — it was hot and prickly, but there was nothing else. That done, he filled the waterbags from the pump.

"You carry one of the waterbags," the gunslinger said. "Wear it around your shoulders — like a fakir carries his snake. See?"

"Yes." The boy looked up at him worshipfully. He slung one of the bags.

"Is it too heavy?"

"No. It's fine."

"Tell me the truth, now. I can't carry you if you get a sunstroke."

"I won't have a sunstroke. I'll be okay."

The gunslinger nodded.

"We're going to the mountains, aren't we?"

"Yes."

They walked out into the steady smash of the sun. Jake, his head as high as the swing of the gunslinger's elbows, walked to his right and a little ahead, the rawhide-wrapped ends of the waterbag hanging nearly to his shins. The gunslinger had crisscrossed two more waterbags across his shoulders and carried the sling of food in his armpit, his left arm holding it against his body.

They passed through the far gate of the way station and found the blurred ruts of the stage track again. They had walked perhaps fifteen minutes when Jake turned around and waved at the two buildings. They seemed to huddle in the titanic space of the desert.

"Goodbye!" Jake cried. "Goodbye!"

They walked. The stage track breasted a frozen sand drumlin, and when the gunslinger looked around, the way station was gone. Once again there was the desert, and that only.

They were three days out of the way station; the mountains were deceptively clear now. They could see the rise of the desert into foothills, the first naked slopes, the bedrock bursting through the skin of the earth in sullen, eroded triumph. Further up, the land gentled off briefly again, and for the first time in months or years the gunslinger could see green — real, living green. Grass, dwarf spruces, perhaps even willows, all fed by snow runoff from further up.

Beyond that the rock took over again, rising in cyclopean, tumbled splendor to the blinding snowcaps. Off to the left, a huge slash showed the way to the smaller, eroded sandstone cliffs and mesas and buttes on the far side. This draw was obscured in the almost continual gray membrane of showers. At night, Jake would sit fascinated for the few minutes before he fell into sleep, watching the brilliant swordplay of the far-off lightning, white and purple, startling in the clarity of the night air.

The boy was fine on the trail. He was tough, but more than that, he seemed to fight exhaustion with a calm and professional reservoir of will which the gunslinger fully appreciated. He did not talk much and he did not ask questions, not even about the jawbone, which the gunslinger turned over and over in his hands during his evening smoke. He caught a sense that the boy felt highly flattered by the gunslinger's companionship — perhaps even exalted by it — and this disturbed him. The boy had been placed in his path — *While you travel with the boy, the man in black travels with your soul in his pocket* — and the fact that Jake was not slowing him down only opened the way to more sinister possibilities.

They passed the symmetrical campfire leavings of the man in black at regular intervals, and it seemed to the gunslinger that these leavings were much fresher now. On the third night, the gunslinger was sure that he could see the distant spark of another campfire, somewhere in the first rising swell of the foothills.

Near two o'clock on the fourth day out from the way station, Jake reeled and almost fell.

"Here, sit down," the gunslinger said.

"No, I'm okay."

"Sit down."

The boy sat obediently. The gunslinger squatted close by, so Jake would be in his shadow.

"Drink."

"I'm not supposed to until — "

"Drink."

The boy drank, three swallows. The gunslinger wet the tail of the blanket, which was lighter now, and applied the damp fabric to the boy's wrists and forehead, which were fever-dry.

"From now on we rest every afternoon at this time. Fifteen minutes. Do you want to sleep?"

"No." The boy looked at him with shame. The gunslinger looked back blandly. In an abstracted way he withdrew one of the bullets from his belt and began to twirl it between his fingers. The boy watched, fascinated.

"That's neat," he said.

The gunslinger nodded. "Sure it is." he paused. "When I was your age, I lived in a walled city, did I tell you that?"

The boy shook his head sleepily.

"Sure. And there was an evil man — "

"The priest?"

"No," the gunslinger said, "but the two of them had some relationship, I think now. Maybe even half-brothers. Marten was a wizard . . . like Merlin. Do they tell of Merlin where you come from, Jake?"

"Merlin and Arthur and the knights of the round table," Jake said dreamily.

The gunslinger felt a nasty jolt go through him. "Yes," he said. "I was very young, . . . "

But the boy was asleep sitting up, his hands folded neatly in his lap.

"When I snap my fingers, you'll wake up. You'll be rested and fresh. Do you understand?"

"Yes."

"Lay over, then."

The gunslinger got makings from his poke and rolled a cigarette. There was something missing. He searched for it in his dilligent, careful way and located it. The missing thing was that maddening sense of hurry, the feeling that he might be left behind at any time, that the trail would die out and he would be left with only a broken piece of string. All that was gone now, and the gunslinger was slowly becoming sure that the man in black wanted to be caught.

What would follow?

The question was too vague to catch his interest. Cuthbert would have found interest in it, lively interest, but Cuthbert was gone, and the gunslinger could only go forward in the way he knew.

He watched the boy as he smoked, and his mind turned back on Cuthbert, who had always laughed — to his death he had gone laughing — and Cort, who never laughed, and on Marten, who sometimes smiled — a thin, silent smile that had its own disquieting gleam . . . like an eye that slips open in the dark and discloses blood. And there had been the falcon, of course. The falcon was named David, after the legend of the boy with the sling. David, he was quite sure, knew nothing but the need for murder, rending, and terror. Like the gunslinger himself. David was no dilettante; he played the center of the court.

Perhaps, though, in some final accounting, David the falcon had been closer to Marten than to anyone else . . . and perhaps his mother, Gabrielle, had known it.

The gunslinger's stomach seemed to rise painfully against his heart, but his face didn't change. He watched the smoke of his cigarette rise into the hot desert air and disappear, and his mind went back.

II

The sky was white, perfectly white, and the smell of rain was in the air. The smell of hedges and growing green was strong and sweet. It was deep spring.

David sat on Cuthbert's arm, a small engine of destruction with bright golden eyes that glared outward at nothing. The rawhide leash attached to his jesses was looped carelessly about Cuthbert's arm.

Cort stood aside from the two boys, a silent figure in patched leather trousers and a green cotton shirt that had been cinched high with his old, wide infantry belt. The green of his shirt merged with the hedges and the rolling turf of the Back Courts, where the ladies had not yet begun to play at Points.

"Get ready," Roland whispered to Cuthbert.

"We're ready," Cuthbert said confidently. "Aren't we, Davey?"

They spoke the low speech, the language of both scullions and squires; the day when they would be allowed to use their own tongue in the presence of others was still far. "It's a beautiful day for it. Can you smell the rain? It's — "

Cort abruptly raised the trap in his hands and let the side fall open. The dove was out and up, trying for the sky in a quick, fluttering blast of its wings. Cuthbert pulled the leash, but he was slow; the hawk was already up and his takeoff was awkward. With a brief twitch of its wings the hawk had recovered. It struck upward, gaining altitude over the dove, moving bullet-swift.

Cort walked over to where the boys stood, casually, and swung his huge and twisted fist at Cuthbert's ear. The boy fell over without a sound, although his lips writhed back from his gums. A trickle of blood flowed slowly from his ear and onto the rich green grass.

"You were slow," he said.

Cuthbert was struggling to his feet. "I'm sorry, Cort. It's just that I — "

Cort swung again, and Cuthbert fell over again. The blood flowed more swiftly now.

"Speak the High Speech," he said softly. His voice was flat, with a slight, drunken rasp. "Speak your act of contrition in the speech of civilization for which better men than you will ever be have died, maggot."

Cuthbert was getting up again. Tears stood brightly in his eyes, but his lips were pressed tightly together in a bright line of hate which did not quiver.

"I grieve," Cuthbert said in a voice of breathless control. "I have forgotten the face of my father, whose guns I hope someday to bear."

"That's right, brat," Cort said. "You'll consider what you did wrong, and bookend your reflections with hunger. No supper. No breakfast."

"Look!" Roland cried. He pointed up.

The hawk had climbed above the soaring dove. It glided for a moment, its stubby, muscular wings outstretched and without movement on the still, white spring air. Then it folded its wings and dropped like a stone. The two bodies came together, and for a moment Roland fancied he could see blood in the air . . . but it might have been his imagination. The hawk gave a brief scream of triumph. The dove fluttered, twisting, to the ground, and Roland ran toward the kill, leaving Cort and the chastened Cuthbert behind him.

The hawk had landed beside its prey and was complacently tearing into its plump white breast. A few feathers seesawed slowly downward.

"David!" The boy yelled, and tossed the hawk a piece of rabbit flesh from his poke. The hawk caught it on the fly, ingested it with an upward shaking of its back and throat, and Roland attempted to re-leash the bird.

The hawk whirled, almost absentmindedly, and ripped skin from Roland's arm in a long, dangling gash. Then it went back to its meal.

With a grunt, Roland looped the leash again, this time catching David's diving, slashing beak on the leather gauntlet he wore. He gave the hawk another piece of meat, then hooded it. Dociley, David climbed onto his wrist.

He stood up proudly, the hawk on his arm.

"What's this?" Cort asked, pointing to the dripping slash on Roland's forearm. The boy stationed himself to receive the blow, locking his throat against any possible cry, but no blow fell.

"He struck me," Roland said.

"You pissed him off," Cort said. "The hawk does not fear you, boy, and the hawk never will. The hawk is God's gunslinger."

Roland merely looked at Cort. He was not an imaginative boy, and if Cort had intended to imply a moral, it was lost on him; he was pragmatic enough to believe that it might have been one of the few foolish statements he had ever heard Cort make.

Cuthbert came up behind them and stuck his tongue out at Cort, safely on his blind side. Roland did not smile, but nodded to him.

"Go in now," Cort said, taking the hawk. He pointed at Cuthbert. "But remember your reflection, maggot. And your fast. Tonight and tomorrow morning."

"Yes," Cuthbert said, stiltedly formal now. "Thank you for this instructive day."

"You learn," Cort said, "but your tongue has a bad habit of lolling from your stupid mouth when your instructor's back is turned. Mayhap the day will come when it and you will learn their respective places." He struck Cuthbert again, this time solidly between the eyes and hard enough so that Roland heard a dull thud — the sound a mallet makes when a scullion taps a keg of beer. Cuthbert fell backward onto the lawn, his eyes cloudy and dazed at first. Then they cleared and he stared burningly up at Cort, his hatred unveiled, a pinprick as bright as the dove's blood in the center of each eye.

Cuthbert nodded and parted his lips in a scarifying smile that Roland had never seen.

"Then there's hope for you," Cort said. "When you think you can, you come for me, maggot."

"How did you know?" Cuthbert said between his teeth.

Cort turned toward Roland so swiftly that Roland almost fell back a step — and then both of them would have been on the grass, decorating the new green with their blood. "I saw it reflected in this maggot's eyes," he said. "Remember it, Cuthbert. Last lesson for today."

Cuthbert nodded again, the same frightening smile on his face. "I grieve," he said. "I have forgotten the face — "

"Cut that shit," Cort said, losing interest. He turned to Roland. "Go on, now. The both of you. If I have to look at your stupid maggot faces any longer I'll puke my guts."

"Come on," Roland said.

Cuthbert shook his head to clear it and got to his feet. Cort was already walking down the hill in his squat, bow-legged stride, looking powerful and somehow prehistoric. The shaved and grizzled spot at the top of his head loomed at a slant, hunched.

"I'll kill the son of a bitch," Cuthbert said, still smiling. A large goose egg, purple and knotted, was rising mystically on his forehead.

"Not you or me," Roland said, suddenly bursting into a grin. "You can have supper in the west kitchen with me. Cook will give us some."

"He'll tell Cort."

"He's no friend of Cort's." Roland said, and then shrugged. "And what if he did?"

Cuthbert grinned back. "Sure. Right. I always wanted to know how the world looked when your head was on backwards and upside down."

They started back together over the green lawns, casting shadows in the fine white springlight.

The cook in the west kitchen was named Hax. He stood huge in foodstained whites, a man with a crude-oil complexion whose ancestry was a quarter black, a quarter yellow, a quarter from the South Islands, now almost forgotten (the world had moved on), and a quarter God knew what. He shuffled about three high-ceilinged steamy rooms like a tractor in low gear, wearing huge, Caliph-like slippers. He was one of those quite rare adults who communicate with small children fairly well and who love them all impartially — not in a sugary way but in a businesslike fashion that may sometimes entail a hug, in the same way that closing a big business deal may call for a handshake. He even loved the boys who had begun The Training, although they were different from other children — not always demonstrative and somehow dangerous, not in an adult way, but rather as if they were ordinary children with a slight touch of madness — and Cuthbert was not the first of Cort's students whom he had fed on the sly. At this moment he stood in front of his huge, rambling electric stove — one of six working appliances left on the whole estate. It was his personal domain, and he stood there watching the two boys bolt the gravied meat scraps he had produced. Behind, before, and all around, cookboys, scullions, and various underlings rushed through the foaming, humid air, rattling pans, stirring stew, slaving over potatoes and vegetables in nether regions. In the dimly lit pantry alcove, a washerwoman with a doughy, miserable face and hair caught up in a rag splashed water around on the floor with a mop.

One of the scullery boys rushed up with a man from the Guards in tow. "This man, he wantchoo, Hax."

"All right." Hax nodded to the Guard, and he nodded back. "You boys," he said. "Go over to Maggie, she'll give you some pie. Then scat."

They nodded and went over to Maggie, who gave them huge wedges of pie on dinner plates . . . but gingerly, as if they were wild dogs that might bite her.

"Let's eat it on the stairs," Cuthbert said.

"All right."

They sat behind a huge, sweating stone colonnade, out of sight of the kitchen, and gobbled their pie with their fingers. It was only moments later that they saw shadows fall on the far curving wall of the wide staircase. Roland grabbed Cuthbert's arm. "Come on," he said. "Someone's coming." Cuthbert looked up, his face surprised and berry-stained.

But the shadows stopped, still out of sight. It was Hax and the man from the Guards. The boys sat where they were. If they moved now, they might be heard.

" . . . the good man," the Guard was saying.

"In Farson?"

"In two weeks," the Guard replied. "Maybe three. You have to come with us. There's a shipment from the freight depot. . . . " A particularly loud crash of pots and pans and a volley of catcalls directed at the hapless potboy who had dropped them blotted out some of the rest; then the boys heard the Guard finish: " . . . poisoned meat."

"Risky."

"Ask not what the good man can do for you — " the Guard began.

" — but what you can do for him," Hax sighed. "Soldier, ask not."

"You know what it could mean," the Guard said quietly.

"Yes. And I know my responsibilities to him; you don't need to lecture me. I love him just as you do."

"All right. The meat will be marked for short-term storage in your coldrooms. But you'll have to be quick. You must understand that."

"There are children in Farson?" The cook asked sadly. It was not really a question.

"Children everywhere," the Guard said gently. "It's the children we — and he — care about."

"Poisoned meat. Such a strange way to care for children." Hax uttered a heavy, whistling sigh. "Will they curdle and hold their bellies and cry for their mammas? I suppose they will."

"It will be like a going to sleep," the Guard said, but his voice was too confidently reasonable.

"Of course," Hax said, and laughed.

"You said it yourself. 'Soldier, ask not.' Do you enjoy seeing children under the rule of the gun, when they could be under his hands, who makes the lion lie down with the lamb?"

Hax did not reply.

"I go on duty in twenty minutes," the Guard said, his voice once more calm. "Give me a joint of mutton and I will pinch one of your girls and make her giggle. When I leave — "

"My mutton will give no cramps to your belly, Robeson."

"Will you . . . " But the shadows moved away and the voices were lost.

I could have killed them, Roland thought, frozen and fascinated. I could have killed them both with my knife, slit their throats like hogs. He looked at his hands, now stained with gravy and berries as well as dirt from the day's lessons.

"Roland."

He looked at Cuthbert. They looked at each other for a long moment in the fragrant semidarkness, and a taste of warm despair rose in Roland's throat. What he felt might have been a sort of death — something as brutal and final as the death of the dove in the white sky over the games field. Hax? He thought, bewildered. Hax who put a poultice on my leg that time? *Hax?* And then his mind snapped closed, cutting the subject off.

What he saw, even in Cuthbert's humorous, intelligent face, was nothing — nothing at all. Cuthbert's eyes were flat with Hax's doom. In Cuthbert's eyes, it had already happened. He had fed them and they had gone to the stairs to eat and then Hax had brought the Guard named Robeson to the wrong corner of the kitchen for their treasonous little *tete-a-tete.* That was all. In Cuthbert's eyes Roland saw that Hax would die for his treason as a viper dies in a pit. That, and nothing else. Nothing at all.

They were gunslinger's eyes.

Roland's father was only just back from the uplands, and he looked out of place amid the drapes and the chiffon fripperies of the main receiving hall that the boy had only lately been granted access to, as a sign of his apprenticeship.

His father was dressed in black jeans and a blue work shirt. His cloak, dusty and streaked, torn to the lining in one place, was slung carelessly over his shoulder with no regard for the way it and he clashed with the elegance of the room. He was desperately thin and the heavy handlebar mustache below his nose seemed to weight his head as he looked down at his son. The guns crisscrossed over the wings of his hips hung at the perfect angle for his hands, the worn sandalwood handles looking dull and sleepy in this languid indoor light.

"The head cook," his father said softly. "Imagine it! The tracks that were blown upland at the railhead. The dead stock in Hendrickson. And perhaps even . . . imagine! Imagine!"

He looked more closely at his son.

"It preys on you."

"Like the hawk," Roland said. "It preys on you." He laughed — at the startling appropriateness of the image rather than at any lightness in the situation.

His father smiled.

"Yes," Roland said. "I guess it . . . it preys on me."

"Cuthbert was with you," his father said. "He will have told his father by now."

"Yes."

"He fed both of you when Cort — "

"Yes."

"And Cuthbert. Does it prey on him, do you think?"

"I don't know." Such an avenue of comparison did not really interest him. He was not concerned with how his feelings compared with those of others.

"It preys on you because you feel you've killed?"

Roland shrugged unwillingly, all at once not content with this probing of his motivations.

"Yet you told. Why?"

The boy's eyes widened. "How could I not? Treason was — "

His father waved a hand curtly. "If you did it for something as cheap as a schoolbook idea, you did it unworthily. I would rather see all of Farson poisoned."

"I didn't!" The words jerked out of him violently. "I wanted to kill him — both of them! Liars! Snakes! They — "

"Go ahead."

"They hurt me," he finished, defiant. "They did something to me. Changed something. I wanted to kill them for it."

His father nodded. "That is worthy. Not moral, but it is not your place to be moral. In fact . . . " He peered at his son. "Morals may always be beyond you. You are not quick, like Cuthbert or Wheeler's boy. It will make you formidable."

The boy, impatient before this, felt both pleased and troubled. "He will — "

"Hang."

The boy nodded. "I want to see it."

Roland the elder threw his head back and roared laughter. "Not as formidable as I thought . . . or perhaps just stupid." He closed his mouth abruptly. An arm shot out like a bolt of lightning and grabbed the boy's upper arm painfully. He grimaced but did not flinch. His father peered at him steadily, and the boy looked back, although it was more difficult than hooding the hawk had been.

"All right," he said, and turned abruptly to go.

"Father?"

"What?"

"Do you know who they were talking about? Do you know who the good man is?"

His father turned back and looked at him speculatively. "Yes. I think I do."

"If you caught him," Roland said in his thoughtful, near-plodding way, "no one else like Cook would have to . . . have to be neck-popped."

His father smiled thinly. "Perhaps not for a while. But in the end, someone always has to have his or her neck popped, as you so quaintly put it. The people demand it. Sooner or later, if there isn't a turncoat, the people make one."

"Yes," Roland said, grasping the concept instantly — it was one he never forgot. "But if you got him — "

"No," his father said flatly.

"Why?"

For a moment his father seemed on the verge of saying why, but he bit it back. "We've talked enough for now, I think. Go out from me."

He wanted to tell his father not to forget his promise when the time came for Hax to step through the trap, but he was sensitive to his father's moods. He suspected his father wanted to fuck. He closed that door quickly. He was aware that his mother and father did that . . . that thing together, and he was reasonably well informed as to what that act was, but the mental picture that always condensed with the thought made him feel both uneasy and oddly guilty. Some years later, Susan would tell him the story of Oedipus, and he would absorb it in quiet thoughtfulness, thinking of the odd and bloody triangle formed by his father, his mother, and by Marten — known in some quarters as the good man. Or perhaps it was a quadrangle, if one wished to add himself.

"Good night, father," Roland said.

"Good night, son," his father said absently, and began unbuttoning his shirt. In his mind, the boy was already gone. Like father, like son.

Gallows Hill was on the Farson Road, which was nicely poetic — Cuthbert might have appreciated this, but Roland did not. He did appreciate the splendidly ominous scaffold which climbed into the brilliantly blue sky, a black and angular silhouette which overhung the coach road.

The two boys had been let out of Morning Exercises — Cort had read the notes from their fathers laboriously, lips moving, nodding here and there. When he finished with them both, he had looked up at the blue-violet dawn sky and had nodded again.

"Wait here," he said, and went toward the leaning stone hut that was his living quarters. He came back with a slice of rough, unleavened bread, broke it in two, and gave half to each.

"When it's over, each of you will put this beneath his shoes. Mind you do exactly as I say, or I'll clout you into next week."

They had not understood until they arrived, riding double on Cuthbert's gelding. They were the first, fully two hours ahead of anyone else and four hours before the hanging, and Gallows Hill stood deserted — except for the rooks and ravens. The birds were everywhere, and of course they were all black. They roosted noisily on the hard, jutting bar that overhung the trap — the armature of death. They sat in a row along the edge of the platform, they jostled for position on the stairs.

"They leave them," Cuthbert muttered. "For the birds."

"Let's go up," Roland said.

Cuthbert looked at him with something like horror. "Do you think — "

Roland cut him off with a gesture of his hands. "We're *years* early. No one will come."

"All right."

They walked slowly toward the gibbet, and the birds took indignant wing, cawing and circling like a mob of angry dispossessed peasants. Their bodies were flat and black against the pure dawnlight of the sky.

For the first time Roland felt the enormity of his responsibility in the matter; this wood was not noble, not part of the awesome machine of Civilization, but merely warped pine covered with splattered white bird droppings. It was splashed everywhere — stairs, railing, platform — and it stank.

The boy turned to Cuthbert with startled, terrified eyes and saw Cuthbert looking back at him with the same expression.

"I can't," Cuthbert whispered. "I can't watch it."

Roland shook his head slowly. There was a lesson here, he realized, not a shining thing but something that was old and rusty and misshapen. It was why their fathers had let them come. And with his usual stubborn and inarticulate doggedness, Roland laid mental hands on whatever it was.

"You can, Bert."

"I won't sleep tonight."

"Then you won't," Roland said, not seeing what that had to do with it.

Cuthbert suddenly seized Roland's hand and looked at him with such mute agony that Roland's own doubt came back, and he wished sickly that they had never gone to the west kitchen that night. His father had been right. Better every man, woman, and child in Farson than this.

But whatever the lesson was, rusty, half-buried thing, he would not let it go or give up his grip on it.

"Let's not go up," Cuthbert said. "We've seen everything."

And Roland nodded reluctantly, feeling his grip on that thing — whatever it was — weaken. Cort, he knew, would have knocked them both sprawling and then forced them up to the platform step by cursing step . . . and sniffing fresh blood back up their noses as they went. Cort would probably have looped new hemp over the yardarm itself and put the noose around each of their necks in turn, would have made them stand on the trap to feel it; and Cort would have been ready to strike them again if either wept or lost

control of his bladder. And Cort, of course, would have
been right. For the first time in his life, Roland found himself hating his own childhood. He wished for the size and
calluses and sureness of age.

He deliberately pried a splinter from the railing and
placed it in his breast pocket before turning away.

"Why did you do that?" Cuthbert asked.

He wished to answer something swaggering: *Oh, the
luck of the gallows* . . . but he only looked at Cuthbert and
shook his head. "Just so I'll have it," he said. "Always have
it."

They walked away from the gallows, sat down, and
waited. In an hour or so the first of them began to gather,
mostly families who had come in broken-down wagons
and shays, carrying their breakfasts with them — hampers
of cold pancakes folded over fillings of wild strawberry
jam. Roland felt his stomach growl hungrily and wondered again, with despair, where the honor and the nobility
of it was. It seemed to him that Hax in his dirty whites, walk-
king around and around his steaming, subterranean kitchen, had more honor than this. He fingered the splinter
from the gallows tree with sick bewilderment. Cuthbert lay
beside him with his face made impassive.

In the end it was not so much, and Roland was glad.
Hax was carried in an open cart, but only his huge girth
gave him away; he had been blindfolded with a wide black
cloth that hung down over his face. A few threw stones, but
most merely continued with their breakfasts.

A gunslinger whom the boy did not know (he was glad
his father had not drawn the lot) led the fat cook carefully
up the steps. Two Guards of the Watch had gone ahead and
stood on either side of the trap. When Hax and the gunslinger reached the top, the gunslinger threw the noosed

rope over the crosstree and then put it over the cook's head, dropping the knot until it lay just below the left ear. The birds had all flown, but Roland knew they were waiting.

"Do you wish to make confession?" the gunslinger asked.

"I have nothing to confess," Hax said. His words carried well, and his voice was oddly dignified in spite of the muffle of cloth which hung over his lips. The cloth ruffled slightly in the faint, pleasant breeze that had blown up. "I have not forgotten my father's face; it has been with me through all."

Roland glanced sharply at the crowd and was disturbed by what he saw there — a sense of sympathy? Perhaps admiration? He would ask his father. When traitors are called heroes (or heroes traitors, he supposed in his frowning way), dark times must have fallen. He wished he understood better. His mind flashed to Cort and the bread Cort had given them. He felt contempt; the day was coming when Cort would serve him. Perhaps not Cuthbert; perhaps Cuthbert would buckle under Cort's steady fire and remain a page or a horseboy (or infinitely worse, a perfumed diplomat, dallying in receiving chambers or looking into bogus crystal balls with doddering kings and princes), but he would not. He knew it.

"Roland?"

"I'm here." He took Cuthbert's hand, and their fingers locked together like iron.

The trap dropped. Hax plummeted through. And in the sudden stillness, there was a sound: that sound an exploding pineknot makes on the hearth during a cold winter night.

But it was not so much. The cook's legs kicked out once in a wide Y; the crowd made a satisfied whistling noise; the Guards of the Watch dropped their military pose and began to gather things up negligently. The gunslinger walked back down the steps slowly, mounted his horse, and rode off, cutting roughly through one gaggle of picknickers, making them scurry.

The crowd dispersed rapidly after that, and in forty minutes the two boys were left alone on the small hill they had chosen. The birds were returning to examine their new prize. One lit on Hax's shoulder and sat there chummily, darting its beak at the bright and shiny hoop Hax had always worn in his right ear.

"It doesn't look like him at all," Cuthbert said.

"Oh, yes, it does," Roland said confidently as they walked toward the gallows, the bread in their hands. Cuthbert looked abashed.

They paused beneath the crosstree, looking up at the dangling, twisting body. Cuthbert reached up and touched one hairy ankle, defiantly. The body started on a new, twisting arc.

Then, rapidly, they broke the bread and spread the crumbs beneath the dangling feet. Roland looked back just once as they rode away. Now there were thousands of birds. The bread — he grasped this only dimly — was symbolic, then.

"It was good," Cuthbert said suddenly. "It . . . I . . . I liked it. I did."

Roland was not shocked by this, although he had not particularly cared for the scene. But he thought he could perhaps understand it.

"I don't know about that," he said, "but it was something. It surely was."

The land did not fall to the good man for another ten years, and by that time he was a gunslinger, his father was dead, he himself had become a matricide — and the world had moved on.

III

"Look," Jake said, pointing upward.

The gunslinger looked up and felt an obscure joint in his back pop. They had been in the foothills two days now, and although the waterskins were almost empty again, it didn't matter now. There would soon be all the water they could drink.

He followed the vector of Jake's finger upward, past the rise of the green plain to the naked and flashing cliffs and gorges above it . . . and on up toward the snowcap itself.

Faint and far, nothing but a tiny dot (it might have been one of those motes that dance perpetually in front of the eyes, except for its constancy), the gunslinger beheld the man in black, moving up the slopes with deadly progress, a minuscule fly on a huge granite wall.

"Is that him?" Jake asked.

The gunslinger looked at the depersonalized mote doing its faraway acrobatics, feeling nothing but a premonition of sorrow.

"That's him, Jake."

"Do you think we'll catch him?"

"Not on this side. On the other. And not if we stand here talking about it."

"They're so high," Jake said. "What's on the other side?"

"I don't know," the gunslinger said. "I don't think anybody does. Maybe they did once. Come on, boy."

They began to move upward again, sending small runnels of pebbles and sand down toward the desert that washed away behind them in a flat bake-sheet that seemed to never end. Above them, far above, the man in black moved up and up and up. It was impossible to see if he looked back. He seemed to leap across impossible gulfs, to scale sheer faces. Once or twice he disappeared, but always they saw him again, until the violet curtain of dusk shut him out of their view. When they made their camp for the evening, the boy spoke little, and the gunslinger wondered if the boy knew what he had already intuited. He thought of Cuthbert's face, hot, dismayed, excited. He thought of the crumbs. He thought of the birds. It ends this way, he thought. Again and again it ends this way. There are quests and roads that lead ever onward, and all of them end in the same place — upon the killing ground.

Except, perhaps, the road to the Tower.

The boy, the sacrifice, his face innocent and very young in the light of their tiny fire, had fallen asleep over his beans. The gunslinger covered him with the horse blanket and then curled up to sleep himself.

THE ORACLE AND THE MOUNTAINS

he boy found the oracle and it almost destroyed him.

Some thin instinct brought the gunslinger up from sleep to the velvet darkness, which had fallen on them at dusk like a shroud of well water. That had been when he and Jake reached the grassy, nearly level oasis above the first rise of tumbled foothills. Even on the hardscrabble below, where they had toiled and fought for every foot in the killer sun, they had been able to hear the sound of crickets rubbing their legs seductively together in the perpetual green of willow groves above them. The gunslinger remained calm in his mind, and the boy had kept up at least the pretense of a façade, and that had made the gunslinger proud. But Jake hadn't been able to hide the wildness in his eyes, which were white and starey, the eyes of a horse scenting water and held back from bolting only by the tenuous chain of its master's mind; like a horse at the point where only understanding, not the spur, could hold it steady. The gunslinger could gauge the need in Jake by the madness the sounds of the crickets bred in his own body. His arms seemed to seek out shale to scrape on, and his knees seemed to beg to be ripped in tiny, maddening, salty gashes.

The sun trampled down on them all the way; even when it turned a swollen, feverish red with sunset, it shone perversely through the knife-cut in the hills off to their left, blinding them and making every teardrop of sweat into a prism of pain.

Then there was grass: at first only yellow scrub, clinging to the bleak soil where the last of the runoff reached with gruesome vitality. Further up there was witchgrass, sparse, then green and rank . . . then the first sweet smell of real grass, mixed with timothy and shaded by the first of the dwarfed firs. There the gunslinger saw an arc of brown movements in the shadows. He drew, fired, and felled the rabbit all before Jake could begin to cry out his surprise. A moment later he had reholstered the gun.

"Here," the gunslinger said. Up ahead the grass deepened into a jungle of green willows that was shocking after the parched sterility of the endless hardpan. There would be a spring, perhaps several of them, and it would be even cooler, but it was better out here in the open. The boy had pushed every step he could push, and there might be sucker-bats in the deeper shadows of the grove. The bats might break the boy's sleep, no matter how deep it was, and if they were vampires, neither of them might awaken . . . at least, not in this world.

The boy said, "I'll get some wood."

The gunslinger smiled. "No, you won't. Sit yourself, Jake." Whose phrase had that been? Some woman.

The boy sat. When the gunslinger got back, Jake was asleep in the grass. A large praying mantis was performing ablutions on the springy stem of Jake's cowlick. The gunslinger set the fire and went after water.

The willow jungle was deeper than he had suspected, and confusing in the failing light. But he found a spring, richly guarded by frogs and peepers. He filled one of their waterskins . . . and paused. The sounds that filled the night awoke an uneasy sensuality in him, a feeling that not even Allie, the woman he had bedded with in Tull, had been able to bring to the fore. Sensuality and fucking are, after all, cousins of the most tenuous relation. He chalked it up to the sudden blinding change from the desert. The softness of the dark seemed nearly decadent.

He returned to the camp and skinned the rabbit while water boiled over the fire. Mixed with the last of their canned food, the rabbit made an excellent stew. He woke Jake and watched him as he ate, bleary but ravenous.

"We stay here tomorrow," the gunslinger said.

"But that man you're after . . . that priest."

"He's no priest. And don't worry. We've got him."

"How do you know that?"

The gunslinger could only shake his head. The knowledge was strong in him . . . but it was not a good knowledge.

After the meal, he rinsed the cans they had eaten from (marveling again at his own water extravagance), and when he turned around, Jake was asleep again. The gunslinger felt the now-familiar rising and falling in his chest that he could only identify with Cuthbert. Cuthbert had been Roland's own age, but he had seemed so much younger.

His cigarette drooped toward the grass, and he tossed it into the fire. He looked at it, the clear yellow burn so different, so much cleaner, from the way the devil-grass burned. The air was wonderfully cool, and he lay down with his back to the fire. Far away, through the gash that led the way into the mountains, he heard the thick mouth of the perpetual thunder. He slept. And dreamed.

Susan, his beloved, was dying before his eyes:

As he watched, his arms held by two villagers on each side, his neck dog-caught in a huge, rusty iron collar, she was dying. Even through the thick stench of the fire Roland could smell the dankness of the pits . . . and he could see the color of his own madness. Susan, lovely girl at the window, horse-drover's daughter.

She was turning black in the flames, her skin cracking open.

"The boy!" She was screaming. "Roland, the boy!"

He whirled, pulling his captors with him. The collar ripped at his neck and he heard the hitching, strangled sounds that were coming from his own throat. There was a sickish-sweet smell of barbecueing meat on the air.

The boy was looking down at him from a window high above the courtyard, the same window where Susan, who had taught him to be a man, had once sat and sung the old songs; "Hey Jude" and "Ease on Down the Road" and "A Hundred Leagues to Banberry Cross." He looked out from the window like the statue of an alabaster saint in a cathedral. His eyes were marble. A spike had been driven through Jake's forehead.

The gunslinger felt the strangling, ripping scream that signaled the beginning of his lunacy pull up from the root of his belly.

"Nnnnnnnnnn — "

Roland grunted a cry as he felt the fire singe him. He sat bolt upright in the dark, still feeling the dream around him, strangling him like the collar he had worn. In his twistings and turnings he had thrown one hand against the dying coals of the fire. He put the hand to his face, feeling the dream flee, leaving only the stark picture of Jake, plasterwhite, a saint for demons.

"Nnnnnnnnnn — "

He glared around at the mystic darkness of the willow grove, both guns out and ready. His eyes were red loopholes in the last glow from the fire.

"Nnnnnn-nnn — "

Jake.

The gunslinger was up and on the run. A bitter circle of moon had risen and he could follow the boy's track in the dew. He ducked under the first of the willows, splashed through the spring, and legged up the far bank, skidding in the dampness (even now his body could relish it). Willow withes slapped at his face. The trees were thicker here, and the moon was blotted out. Treetrunks rose in lurching shadows. The grass, now knee-high, slapped against him. Half-rotted dead branches reached for his shins, his *cojones.* He paused for a moment, lifting his head and scenting at the air. A ghost of a breeze helped him. The boy did not smell good, of course; neither of them did. The gunslinger's nostrils flared like those of an ape. The odor of sweat was faint, oily, unmistakable. He crashed over a deadfall of grass and bramble and downed branches, sprinted down a tunnel of overhanging willow and sumac. Moss struck his shoulders. Some clung in sighing gray tendrils.

He clawed through a last barricade of willows and came to a clearing that looked up at the stars and the highest peak of the range, gleaming skull-white at an impossible altitude.

There was a ring of tall, black stones which looked like some sort of surreal animal-trap in the moonlight. In the center was a table of stone . . . an altar. Very old, rising out of the ground on a powerful arm of basalt.

The boy stood before it, trembling back and forth. His hands shook at his sides as if infused with static electricity. The gunslinger called his name sharply, and Jake responded with that inarticulate sound of negation. The faint smear of face, almost hidden by the boy's left shoulder, looked both terrified and exalted. And there was something else.

The gunslinger stepped inside the ring and Jake screamed, recoiling and throwing up his arms. Now his face could be seen clearly, and indexed. The gunslinger saw fear and terror warring with an almost excruciating grimace of pleasure.

The gunslinger felt it touch him — the spirit of the

oracle, the succubus. His loins were suddenly filled with rose light, a light that was soft yet hard. He felt his head twisting, his tongue thickening and becoming excruciatingly sensitive to even the spittle that coated it.

He did not think when he pulled the half-rotted jawbone from the pocket where he had carried it since he found it in the lair of the Speaking Demon at the way station. He did not think, but it did not frighten him to operate on pure instinct. He held the jawbone's frozen, prehistoric grin up in front of him, holding his other arm out stiffly, first and last fingers poked out in the ancient forked talisman, the ward against the evil eye.

The current of sensuality was whipped away from him like a drape.

Jake screamed again.

The gunslinger walked to him, and held the jawbone in front of Jake's warring eyes. A wet sound of agony. The boy tried to pull his gaze away, could not. And suddenly both eyes rolled up to show the whites. Jake collapsed. His body struck the earth limply, one hand almost touching the altar. The gunslinger dropped to one knee and picked him up. He was amazingly light, as dehydrated as a November leaf from their long walk through the desert.

Around him Roland could feel the presence that dwelt in the circle of stones, whirring with a jealous anger — its prize had been taken from it. When the gunslinger passed out of the circle, the sense of frustrated jealousy faded. He carried Jake back to their camp. By the time they got there, the boy's twitching unconsciousness had become deep sleep. The gunslinger paused for a moment above the gray ruin of the fire. The moonlight on Jake's face reminded him again of a church saint, alabaster purity all unknown. He suddenly hugged the boy, knowing that he loved him. And it seemed that he could almost feel the laughter from the man in black, someplace far above them.

Jake was calling him; that was how he awoke. He had tied the boy firmly to one of the tough bushes that grew nearby, and the boy was hungry and upset. By the sun, it was almost nine-thirty.

"Why'd you tie me up?" Jake asked indignantly as the gunslinger loosened the thick knots in the blanket. "I wasn't going to run away!"

"You did run away," the gunslinger said, and the expression on Jake's face made him smile. "I had to go out and get you. You were sleepwalking."

"I was?" Jake looked at him suspiciously.

The gunslinger nodded and suddenly produced the jawbone. He held it in front of Jake's face and Jake flinched away from it, raising his arm.

"See?"

Jake nodded, bewildered.

"I have to go off for a while now. I may be gone the whole day. So listen to me, boy. It's important. If sunset comes and I'm not back — "

Fear flashed on Jake's face. "You're leaving me!"

The gunslinger only looked at him.

"No," Jake said after a moment. "I guess you're not."

"I want you to stay right here while I'm gone. And if you feel strange — funny in any way — you pick up this bone and hold it in your hands."

Hate and disgust crossed Jake's face, mixed with bewilderment. "I couldn't. I . . . I just couldn't."

"You can. You may have to. Especially after midday. It's important. Dig?"

"Why do you have to go away?" Jake burst out.

"I just do."

The gunslinger caught another fascinating glimpse of the steel that lay under the boy's surface, as enigmatic as the story he had told about coming from a city where the buildings were so tall they actually scraped the sky.

"All right," Jake said.

The gunslinger laid the jawbone carefully on the ground next to the ruins of the fire, where it grinned up through the grass like some eroded fossil that has seen the light of day after a night of five thousand years. Jake would not look at it. His face was pale and miserable. The gunslinger wondered if it would profit them for him to put the boy to sleep and question him, but he decided there would be little gain. He knew well enough that the spirit of the stone circle was surely a demon, and very likely an oracle as well. A demon with no shape, only a kind of unformed sexual glare with the eye of prophecy. He wondered sardonically if it might not be the soul of Sylvia Pittston, the giant woman whose religious huckstering had led to the final showdown in Tull . . . but knew it was not. The stones in the circle had been ancient, this particular demon's territory staked out long before the earliest shade of pre-history. But the gunslinger knew the forms of speaking quite well and did not think the boy would have to use the jawbone mojo. The voice and mind of the oracle would be more than occupied with him. And the gunslinger needed to know things, in spite of the risk . . . and the risk was high. For both Jake and himself, he needed desperately to know.

The gunslinger opened his tobacco poke and pawed through it, pushing the dry strands of leaf aside until he came to a minuscule object wrapped in a fragment of white paper. He hefted it in his hand, looking absently up at the sky. Then he unwrapped it and held the contents — a tiny white pill with edges that had been much worn with traveling — in his hand.

Jake looked at it curiously. "What's that?"

The gunslinger uttered a short laugh. "The philosopher's stone," he said. "The story that Cort used to tell us was that the Old Gods pissed over the desert and made mescaline."

Jake only looked puzzled.

"A drug," the gunslinger said. "But not one that puts you to sleep. One that wakes you up all the way for a little while."

"Like LSD," the boy agreed instantly and then looked puzzled.

"What's that?"

"I don't know," Jake said. "It just popped out. I think it came from . . . you know, before."

The gunslinger nodded, but he was doubtful. He had never heard of mescaline referred to as LSD, not even in Marten's old books.

"Will it hurt you?" Jake asked.

"It never has," the gunslinger said, conscious of the evasion.

"I don't like it."

"Never mind."

The gunslinger squatted in front of the waterskin, took a mouthful, and swallowed the pill. As always, he felt an immediate reaction in his mouth; it seemed overloaded with saliva. He sat down before the dead fire.

"When does something happen to you?" Jake asked.

"Not for a little while. Be quiet."

So Jake was quiet, watching with open suspicion as the gunslinger went calmly about the ritual of cleaning his guns.

He reholstered them and said, "Your shirt, Jake. Take it off and give it to me."

Jake pulled his faded shirt reluctantly over his head and gave it to the gunslinger.

The gunslinger produced a needle that had been threaded into the side-seam of his jeans, and thread from an empty cartridge-loop in his gunbelt. He began to sew up a long rip in one of the sleeves of the boy's shirt. As he finished and handed the shirt back, he felt the mesc beginning to take hold — there was a tightening in his stomach and a feeling that all the muscles in his body were being cranked up a notch.

"I have to go," he said, getting up.

The boy half rose, his face a shadow of concern, and then he settled back. "Be careful," he said. "Please."

"Remember the jawbone," the gunslinger said. He put his hand on Jake's head as he went by and touseled the corn-colored hair. The gesture startled him into a short laugh. Jake watched after him with a troubled smile until he was gone into the willow jungle.

The gunslinger walked deliberately toward the circle of stones, pausing once to get a cool drink from the spring. He could see his own reflection in a tiny pool edged with moss and lilypads, and he looked at himself for a moment, as fascinated as Narcissus. The mind-reaction was beginning to settle in, slowing down his chain of thought by seeming to increase the connotations of every idea and every bit of sensory input. Things began to take on weight and thickness that had been heretofore invisible. He paused, getting to his feet again, and looked through the tangled snarl of willows. Sunlight slanted through in a golden, dusty bar, and he watched the interplay of motes and tiny flying things for a moment before going on.

The drug often had disturbed him: his ego was too strong (or perhaps just too simple) to enjoy being eclipsed and peeled back, made a target for more sensitive emotions — they tickled at him like a cat's whiskers. But this time he felt fairly calm. That was good.

He stepped into the clearing and walked straight into the circle. He stood, letting his mind run free. Yes, it was coming harder now, faster. The grass screamed green at him; it seemed that if he bent over and rubbed his hands in it he would stand up with green paint all over his fingers and palms. He resisted a puckish urge to try the experiment.

But there was no voice from the oracle. No sexual stirring.

He went to the altar, stood beside it for a moment. Coherent thought was now almost impossible. His teeth felt strange in his head. The world held too much light. He climbed up on the altar and lay back. His mind was becoming a jungle full of strange thought-plants that he had never seen or suspected before, a willow-jungle that had grown up around a mescaline spring. The sky was water and he hung suspended over it. The thought gave him a vertigo that seemed faraway and unimportant.

A line of old poetry occurred to him, not a nursery verse now, no; his mother had feared the drugs and the necessity of them (as she had feared Cort and the necessity for this beater of boys); this verse came from one of the Dens to the north of the desert, where men still lived among the machines that usually didn't work . . . and which sometimes ate the men when they did. The lines played again and again, reminding him (in an unconnected way that was typical of the mescaline rush) of snow falling in a globe he had owned as a child, mystic and half fantastical:

> *Beyond the reach of human range*
> *A drop of hell, a touch of strange . . .*

The trees which overhung the altar contained faces. He watched them with abstracted fascination: Here was a dragon, green and twitching. Here a wood-nymph with beckoning branch arms. Here a living skull overgrown with slime. Faces. Faces.

The grasses of the clearing suddenly whipped and bent.

I come.

I come.

Vague stirrings within his flesh. How far I have come,

he thought. From couching with Susan in sweet hay to this.

She pressed over him, a body made of the wind, a breast of sudden fragrant jasmine, rose, and honeysuckle.

"Make your prophecy," he said. His mouth felt full of metal.

A sigh. A faint sound of weeping. The gunslinger's genitals felt drawn and hard. Over him and beyond the faces in the leaves, he could see the mountains — hard and brutal and full of teeth.

The body moved against him, struggled with him. He felt his hands curl into fists. She had sent him a vision of Susan. It was Susan above him, lovely Susan at the window, waiting for him with her hair spilled down her back and over her shoulders. He tossed his head, but her face followed.

Jasmine, rose, honeysuckle, old hay . . . the smell of love. Love me.

"Speak prophecy," he said.

Please, the oracle wept. *Don't be cold. It is always so cold here —*

Hands slipping over his flesh, manipulating, lighting him on fire. Pulling him. Drawing. A black crevice. The ultimate wanton. Wet and warm —

No. Dry. Cold. Sterile.

Have a touch of mercy, gunslinger. Ah, please, I beg your favor! Mercy!

Would you have mercy on the boy?

What boy? I know no boy. It's not boys I need. O please.

Jasmine, rose, honeysuckle. Dry hay with its ghost of summer clover. Oil decanted from ancient urns. A riot for flesh.

"After," he said.

Now. Please. Now.

He let his mind coil out at her, the antithesis of emotion. The body that hung over him froze and seemed to scream.

There was a brief, vicious tug-of-war between his temples — his mind was the rope, gray and fibrous. For long moments there was no sound but the quiet hush of his breathing and the faint breeze which made the green faces in the trees shift, wink, and grimace. No bird sang.

Her hold loosened. Again there was the sound of sobbing. It would have to be quick, or she would leave him. To stay now meant attenuation; perhaps her own kind of death. Already he felt her drawing away to leave the circle of stones. Wind rippled the grass in tortured patterns.

"Prophecy," he said — a bleak noun.

A weeping, tired sigh. He could almost have granted the mercy she begged, but — there was Jake. He would have found Jake dead or insane if he had been any later last night.

Sleep, then.

"No."

Then half-sleep.

The gunslinger turned his eyes up to the faces in the leaves. A play was being enacted there for his amusement. Worlds rose and fell before him. Empires were built across shining sands where forever machines toiled in abstract electronic frenzies. Empires declined and fell. Wheels that had spun like silent liquid moved more slowly, began to squeak, began to scream, stopped. Sand choked the stainless steel gutters of concentric streets below dark skies full of stars like beds of cold jewels. And through it all, a dying wind of change blew, bringing with it the cinnamon smell of late October. The gunslinger watched as the world moved on.

And half-slept.

Three. This is the number of your fate.

Three?

Yes, three is mystic. Three stands at the heart of the mantra.

Which three?

'We see in part, and thus is the mirror of prophecy darkened.'

Tell me what you can.

The first is young, dark-haired. He stands on the brink of robbery and murder. A demon has infested him. The name of the demon is HEROIN.

Which demon is that? I know it not, even from nursery stories.

'We see in part, and thus is the mirror of prophecy darkened.' There are other worlds, gunslinger, and other demons. These waters are deep.

The second?

She comes on wheels. Her mind is iron but her heart and eyes are soft. I see no more.

The third?

In chains.

The man in black? Where is he?

Near. You will speak with him.

Of what will we speak?

The Tower.

The boy? Jake?

. . .

Tell me of the boy!

The boy is your gateway to the man in black. The man in black is your gate to the three. The three are your way to the Dark Tower.

How? How can that be? Why must it be?

'We see in part, and thus is the mirror — '

God damn you.

No god damned me.

"Don't patronize me, Thing. I'm stronger than you.

. . .

What do they call you, then? Star-slut? Whore of the Winds?

Some live on love that comes to the ancient places . . . even

in these sad and evil times. Some, gunslinger, live on blood. Even,
I understand, on the blood of young boys.

May he not be spared?

Yes.

How?

Cease, gunslinger. Strike your camp and turn west. In the
west there is still a need for men who live by the bullet.

I am sworn by my father's guns and by the treachery
of Marten.

Marten is no more. The man in black has eaten his soul. This
you know.

I am sworn.

Then you are damned.

Have your way with me, bitch.

Eagerness.

The shadow swung over him, enfolded him. Suddenly
ecstasy broken only by a galaxy of pain, as faint and bright
as ancient stars gone red with collapse. Faces came to him
unbidden at the climax of their coupling: Sylvia Pittston,
Alice, the woman from Tull, Susan, Aileen, a hundred
others.

And finally, after an eternity, he pushed her away from
him, once again in his right mind, bone-weary and dis-
gusted.

No! It isn't enough! It —

"Let me be," the gunslinger said. He sat up and almost
fell off the altar before regaining his feet. She touched him
tentatively

(honeysuckle, jasmine, sweet attar)

and he pushed her violently, falling to his knees.

He staggered up and made his drunken way to the
perimeter of the circle. He staggered through, feeling a
huge weight fall from his shoulders. He drew a shuddering, weeping breath. As he started away he could feel

her standing at the bars of her prison, watching him go
from her. He wondered how long it might be before someone else crossed the desert and found her, hungry and
alone. For a moment he felt dwarfed by the possibilities
of time.

"You're sick!"

Jake stood up fast when the gunslinger shambled back
through the last trees and came into camp. Jake had been
huddled by the ruins of the tiny fire, the jawbone across his
knees, gnawing disconsolately on the bones of the rabbit.
Now he ran toward the gunslinger with a look of distress
that made Roland feel the full, ugly weight of a coming betrayal — one he sensed which might only be the first of many.

"No," he said. "Not sick. Just tired. I'm whipped." He
gestured absently at the jawbone. "You can throw that away."

Jake threw it quickly and violently, rubbing his hands
across his shirt after doing it.

The gunslinger sat down — almost fell down — feeling
the aching joints and the pummeled, thick mind that was
the unlovely afterglow of mescaline. His crotch also pulsed
with a dull ache. He rolled a cigarette with careful, unthinking slowness. Jake watched. The gunslinger had a sudden impulse to tell him what he had learned, then thrust the
idea away with horror. He wondered if a part of him — mind
or soul — might not be disintegrating.

"We sleep here tonight," the gunslinger said. "Tomorrow we climb. I'll go out a little later and see if I can't
shoot something for supper. I've got to sleep now. Okay?"

"Sure."

The gunslinger nodded and lay back. When he woke
up the shadows were long across the small grass clearing.
"Build up the fire," he told Jake and tossed him his flint
and steel. "Can you use that?"

"Yes, I think so."

The gunslinger walked toward the willow grove and then turned left, skirting it. At a place where the ground opened out and upward in heavy open grass, he stepped back into the shadows and stood silently. Faintly, clearly, he could hear the *clik-clink-clik-clink* of Jake striking sparks. He stood without moving for ten minutes, fifteen, twenty. Three rabbits came, and the gunslinger pulled leather. He took down the two plumpest, skinned them and gutted them, brought them back to the camp. Jake had the fire going and the water was already steaming over it.

The gunslinger nodded to him. "That's a good piece of work."

Jake flushed with pleasure and silently handed back the flint and steel.

While the stew cooked, the gunslinger used the last of the light to go back into the willow grove. Near the first pool he began to hack at the tough vines that grew near the water's marshy verge. Later, as the fire burned down to coals and Jake slept, he would plait them into ropes that might be of some limited use later. But he did not think somehow that the climb would be a particularly difficult one. He felt a sense of fate that he no longer even considered odd.

The vines bled green sap over his hands as he carried them back to where Jake waited.

They were up with the sun and packed in half an hour. The gunslinger hoped to shoot another rabbit in the meadow as they fed, but time was short and no rabbit showed itself. The bundle of their remaining food was now so small and light that Jake carried it easily. He had toughened up, this boy; you could see it.

The gunslinger carried their water, freshly drawn from one of the springs. He looped his three vine ropes

around his belly. They gave the circle of stones a wide berth
(the gunslinger was afraid the boy might feel a recurrence
of fear, but when they passed above it on a stony rise, Jake
only offered it a passing glance and then looked at a bird
that hovered upwind). Soon enough, the trees began to lose
their height and lushness. Trunks were twisted and roots
seemed to struggle with the earth in a tortured hunt for
moisture.

"It's all so old," Jake said glumly when they paused for
a rest. "Isn't there anything young?"

The gunslinger smiled and gave Jake an elbow. "You
are," he said.

"Will it be a hard climb?"

The gunslinger looked at him, curious. "The mountains are high. Don't you think it will be a hard climb?"

Jake looked back at him, his eyes clouded, puzzled.
"No."

They went on.

The sun climbed to its zenith, seemed to hang there
more briefly than it ever had during the desert crossing,
and then passed on, giving them back their shadows. Shelves
of rock protruded from the rising land like the arms of
giant easychairs buried in the earth. The scrub grass turned
yellow and sere. Finally they were faced with a deep, chim-
neylike crevasse in their path and they scaled a short, peel-
ing rise of rock to get around and above it. The ancient
granite had faulted on lines that were steplike, and as they
had both intuited, the climb was an easy one. They paused
on the four-foot-wide scarp at the top and looked back over
the falling land to the desert, which curled around the upland like a huge yellow paw. Further off it gleamed at them
in a white shield that dazzled the eye, receding into dim
waves of rising heat. The gunslinger felt faintly amazed at
the realization that this desert had nearly murdered him.

From where they stood, in a new coolness, the desert certainly appeared momentous, but not deadly.

They turned back to the business of the climb, scrambling over jackstraw falls of rock and crouch-walking up inclined planes of stone shot with glitters of quartz and mica. The rock was pleasantly warm to the touch, but the air was definitely cooler. In the late afternoon the gunslinger heard the faint sound of thunder. The rising line of the mountains obscured the sight of the rain on the other side, however.

When the shadows began to turn purple, they camped in the overhang of a jutting brow of rock. The gunslinger anchored their blanket above and below, fashioning a kind of shanty lean-to. They sat at the mouth of it, watching the sky spread a cloak over the world. Jake dangled his feet over the drop. The gunslinger rolled his evening smoke and eyed Jake half humorously. "Don't roll over in your sleep," he said, "or you may wake up in hell."

"I won't," Jake replied seriously. "My mother says — " He broke it off.

"She says what?"

"That I sleep like a dead man," Jake finished. He looked at the gunslinger, who saw that the boy's mouth was trembling as he strove to keep back tears — *only a boy,* he thought, and pain smote him, like the icepick that too much cold water can sometimes plant in the forehead. *Only a boy. Why?* Silly question. When a boy, wounded in body or spirit, called that question out to Cort, that ancient, scarred battle-engine whose job it was to teach the sons of gunslingers the beginning of what they had to know, Cort would answer: *Why is a crooked letter and can't be made straight . . . never mind why, just get up, pus-head! Get up! The day's young!*

"Why am I here?" Jake asked. "Why did I forget everything from before?"

"Because the man in black has drawn you here," the gunslinger said. "And because of the Tower. The Tower stands at a kind of . . . power-nexus. In time."

"I don't understand that!"

"Nor do I," the gunslinger said. "But something has been happening. Just in my own time. 'The world has moved on,' we say . . . we've always said. But it's moving on faster now. Something has happened to time."

They sat in silence. A breeze, faint but with an edge, picked at their legs. Somewhere it made a hollow *whooooo* in a rock fissure.

"Where do you come from?" Jake asked.

"From a place that no longer exists. Do you know the Bible?"

"Jesus and Moses. Sure."

The gunslinger smiled. "That's right. My land had a Biblical name — New Canaan, it was called. The land of milk and honey. In the Bible's Canaan, there were supposed to be grapes so big that men had to carry them on sledges. We didn't grow them that big, but it was a sweet land."

"I know about Ulysses," Jake said hesitantly. "Was he in the Bible?"

"Maybe," the gunslinger said. "The Book is lost now — all except the parts I was forced to memorize."

"But the others — "

"No others," the gunslinger said. "I'm the last."

A tiny wasted moon began to rise, casting its slitted gaze down into the tumble of rocks where they sat.

"Was it pretty? Your country . . . your land?"

"It was beautiful," the gunslinger said absently. "There were fields and rivers and mists in the morning. But that's only pretty. My mother used to say that . . . and that the only real beauty is order and love and light."

Jake made a noncommittal noise.

The gunslinger smoked and thought of how it had been — the nights in the huge central hall, hundreds of richly clad figures moving through the slow, steady waltz steps or the faster, light ripples of the *pol-kam*, Aileen on his arm, her eyes brighter than the most precious gems, the light of the crystal-enclosed electric lights making highlights in the newly done hair of the courtesans and their half-cynical amours. The hall had been huge, an island of light whose age was beyond telling, as was the whole Central Place, which was made up of nearly a hundred stone castles. It had been twelve years since he had seen it, and leaving for the last time, Roland had ached as he turned his face away from it and began his first cast for the trail of the man in black. Even then, twelve years ago, the walls had fallen, weeds grew in the courtyards, bats roosted amongst the great beams of the central hall, and the galleries echoed with the soft swoop and whisper of swallows. The fields where Cort had taught them archery and gunnery and falconry were gone to hay and timothy and wild vines. In the huge and echoey kitchen where Hax had once held his own fuming and aromatic court, a grotesque colony of Slow Mutants nested, peering at him from the merciful darkness of pantries and shadowed pillars. The warm steam that had been filled with the pungent odors of roasting beef and pork had been transmuted to the clammy damp of moss and huge white toadstools grew in corners where not even the Slow Muties dared to encamp. The huge oak subcellar bulkhead stood open, and the most poignant smell of all had issued from that, and odor that seemed to symbolize with a flat finality all the hard facts of disolution and decay: the high sharp odor of wine gone to vinegar. It had been no struggle to turn his face to the south and leave it behind — but it had hurt his heart.

"Was there a war?" Jake asked.

"Even better," the gunslinger said and pitched the last smoldering ember of his cigarette away. "There was a revolution. We won every battle, and lost the war. No one won the war, unless maybe it was the scavengers. There must have been rich pickings for years after."

"I wish I'd lived there," Jake said wistfully.

"It was another world," the gunslinger said. "Time to turn in."

The boy, now only a dim shadow, turned on his side and curled up with the blanket tossed loosely over him. The gunslinger sat sentinel over him for perhaps an hour after, thinking his long, sober thoughts. Such meditation was a new thing for him, novel, sweet in a melancholy sort of way, but still utterly without practical value: there was no solution to the problem of Jake other than the one the Oracle had offered — and that was simply not possible. There might have been tragedy in the situation, but the gunslinger did not see that; he saw only the predestination that had always been there. And finally, his more natural character reasserted itself and he slept deeply, with no dreams.

The climb became grimmer on the following day as they continued to angle toward the narrow V of the pass through the mountains. The gunslinger pushed slowly, still with no sense of hurry. The dead stone beneath their feet left no trace of the man in black, but the gunslinger knew he had been this way before them — and not only from the path of his climb as he and Jake had observed him, tiny and bug-like, from the foothills. His aroma was printed on every cold downdraft of air. It was an oily, sardonic odor, as bitter. to his nose as the aroma of devil-grass.

Jake's hair had grown much longer, and it curled slightly at the base of his sunburned neck. He climbed tough, moving with sure-footedness and no apparent acrophobia as they crossed gaps or scaled their way up ledged facings. Twice already he had gone up in places the gunslinger could not have managed. Jake had anchored one of the ropes so that the gunslinger could climb up hand over hand.

The following morning they climbed through a coldly damp snatch of cloud that began blotting out the tumbled slopes below them. Patches of hard, granulated snow began to appear nestled in some of the deeper pockets of stone. It glittered like quartz and its texture was as dry as sand. That afternoon they found a single footprint in one of these snow-patches. Jake stared at it for a moment with awful fascination, then looked up frightfully, as if expecting to see the man in black materialize into his own footprint. The gunslinger tapped him on the shoulder then and pointed ahead. "Go. The day's getting old."

Later, they made camp in the last of the daylight on a wide, flat ledge to the east and north of the cut that slanted into the heart of the mountains. The air was frigid; they could see the puffs of their breath, and the humid sound of thunder in the red-and-purple afterglow of the day was surreal, slightly lunatic.

The gunslinger thought the boy might begin to question him, but there were no questions from Jake. The boy fell almost immediately into sleep. The gunslinger followed his example. He dreamed again of the dark place in the earth, the dungeon, and again of Jake as an alabaster saint with a nail through his forehead. He awoke with a gasp, instinctively reaching for the jawbone that was no longer there, expecting to feel the grass of that ancient grove. He felt rock instead, and the cold thinness of altitude in his lungs. Jake was asleep beside him, but his sleep was not easy: he twisted and mumbled inarticulate words to himself, chasing his own phantoms. The gunslinger laid over uneasily, and slept again.

They were another week before they reached the end of the beginning — for the gunslinger, a twisted prologue of twelve years, from the final crash of his native place and the gathering of the other three. For Jake, the gateway had been a strange death in another world. For the gunslinger it had been a stranger death yet — the endless hunt for the man in black through a world with neither map nor memory. Cuthbert and the others were gone, all of them gone: Randolph, Jamie de Curry, Aileen, Susan, Marten (yes, they had dragged him down, and there had been gunplay, and even that grape had been bitter). Until finally only three remained of the old world, three like dreadful cards from a terrible deck of tarot cards: gunslinger, man in black, and the Dark Tower.

A week after Jake saw the footstep, they faced the man in black for a brief moment of time. In that moment, the gunslinger felt he could almost understand the gravid implication of the Tower itself, for that moment seemed to stretch out forever.

They continued southwest, reaching a point perhaps halfway through the Cyclopean mountain range, and just as the going seemed about to become really difficult for the first time (above them, seeming to lean out, the icy ledges and screaming buttes made the gunslinger feel an unpleasant reverse vertigo), they began to descend again along the side of the narrow pass. An angular, zigzagging path led them toward a canyon floor where an ice-edged stream boiled with slaty, headlong power from higher country still.

On that afternoon the boy paused and looked back at the gunslinger, who had paused to wash his face in the stream.

"I smell him," Jake said.

"So do I."

Ahead of them the mountain threw up its final defense — a huge slab of insurmountable granite facing that climbed into cloudy infinity. At any moment the gunslinger expected a twist in the stream to bring them upon a high waterfall and the insurmountable smoothness of rock — dead end. But the air here had that odd magnifying quality that is common to high places, and it was another day before they reached that great granite face.

The gunslinger began to feel the dreadful tug of anticipation again, the feeling that it was all finally in his grasp. Near the end, he had to fight himself to keep from breaking into a trot.

"Wait!" The boy had stopped suddenly. They faced a sharp elbow-bend in the stream; it boiled and frothed with high energy around the eroded hang of a giant sandstone boulder. All that morning they had been in the shadow of the mountains as the canyon narrowed.

Jake was trembling violently and his face had gone pale. "What's the matter?"

"Let's go back," Jake whispered. "Let's go back quick."

The gunslinger's face was wooden.

"Please?" The boy's face was drawn, and his jawline shook with suppressed agony. Through the heavy blanket of stone they still heard thunder, as steady as machines in the earth. The slice of sky they could see had itself assumed a turbulent, gothic gray above them as warm and cold currents met and warred.

"Please, *please!*" The boy raised a fist, as if to strike the gunslinger's chest.

"No."

The boy's face took on wonder. "You're going to kill me. He killed me the first time and you are going to kill me now."

The gunslinger felt the lie on his lips. He spoke it:

"You'll be all right." And a greater lie. "I'll take care."

Jake's face went gray, and he said no more. He put an unwilling hand out, and he and the gunslinger went around the elbow-bend. They came face to face with that final rising wall and the man in black.

He stood no more than twenty feet above them, just to the right of the waterfall that crashed and spilled from a huge ragged hole in the rock. Unseen wind rippled and tugged at his hooded robe. He held a staff in one hand. The other hand he held out to them in a mocking gesture of welcome. He seemed a prophet, and below that rushing sky, mounted on a ledge of rock, a prophet of doom, his voice the voice of Jeremiah.

"Gunslinger! How well you fulfill the prophecies of old! Good day and good day and good day!" He laughed, the sound echoing ever over the bellow of the falling water.

Without a thought and seemingly without a click of motor relays, the gunslinger had drawn his pistols. The boy cowered to his right and behind, a small shadow.

Roland fired three times before he could gain control of his traitor hands — the echoes bounced their bronze tones against the rock valley that rose around them, over the sound of the wind and water.

A spray of granite puffed over the head of the man in black; a second to the left of his hood; a third to the right. He had missed cleanly all three times.

The man in black laughed — a full, hearty laugh that seemed to challenge the receding echo of gunshots. "Would you kill all your answers so easily, gunslinger?"

"Come down," the gunslinger said. "Answers all around."

Again that huge, derisive laugh. "It's not your bullets I fear, Roland. It's your idea of answers that scares me."

"Come down."

"The other side, I think," the man in black said. "On the other side we will hold much council."

His eyes flicked to Jake and he added:

"Just the two of us."

Jake flinched away from him with a small, whining cry, and the man in black turned, his robe swirling in the gray air like a batwing. He disappeared into the cleft in the rock from which the water spewed at full force. The gunslinger exercised grim will and did not send a bullet after him — *would you kill all your answers so easily, gunslinger?*

There was only the sound of wind and water, sounds that had been in this place of desolation for a thousand years. Yet the man in black had been here. After these twelve years, Roland had seen him close-up, spoken to him. And the man in black had laughed at him.

On the other side we will hold much council.

The boy looked up at him with dumbly submissive sheep's eyes, his body trembling. For a moment the gunslinger saw the face of Alice, the girl from Tull, superimposed over Jake's, the scar standing out on her forehead like a mute accusation, and felt brute loathing for them both (it would not occur to him until much later that both the scar on Alice's forehead and the nail he saw spiked through Jake's forehead in his dreams were in the same place). Jake seemed to catch a whiff of his thought and a moan was dragged from his throat. But it was short; he twisted his lips shut over it. He held the makings of a fine man, perhaps a gunslinger in his own right if given time.

Just the two of us.

The gunslinger felt a great and unholy thirst in some deep unknown pit of his body, a thirst no wine could touch. Worlds trembled, almost within reach of his fingers, and in some instinctual way he strove not to be corrupted, knowing in his colder mind that such strife was vain and always would be.

It was noon. He looked up, letting the cloudy, unsettled daylight shine for the last time on the all-too-vulnerable sun of his own righteousness. No one ever really pays for it in silver, he thought. The price of any evil — necessary or otherwise — comes due in flesh.

"Come with me or stay," the gunslinger said.

The boy only looked at him mutely. And to the gunslinger, in that final and vital moment of uncoupling from a moral principle, he ceased to be Jake and became only the boy, an impersonality to be moved and used.

Something screamed in the windy stillness; he and the boy both heard.

The gunslinger began, and after a moment Jake came after. Together they climbed the tumbled rock beside the steely-cold falls, and stood where the man in black had stood before them. And together they entered in where he had disappeared. The darkness swallowed them.

THE
SLOW
MUTANTS

The gunslinger spoke slowly to Jake in the rising and falling inflections of a dream:

"There were three of us: Cuthbert, Jamie, and I. We weren't supposed to be there, because none of us had passed from the time of children. If we had been caught, Cort would have striped us. But we weren't. I don't think any of the ones that went before us were caught, either. Boys must put on their fathers' pants in private, strut them in front of the mirror, and then sneak them back on their hangers; it was like that. The father pretends he doesn't notice the new way they are hung up, or the traces of boot-polish mustaches still under their noses. Do you see?"

The boy said nothing. He had said nothing since they had relinquished the daylight. The gunslinger had talked hectically, feverishly, to fill his silence. He had not looked back at the lights as they passed into the lightlessness beneath the mountains, but the boy had. The gunslinger had read the failing of day in the soft mirror of Jake's cheek: Now faint rose; now milk-glass; now pallid silver; now the last dusk-glow touch of evening; now nothing. The gunslinger had struck a false light and they had gone on.

Now they were camped. No echo from the man in black returned to them. Perhaps he had stopped to rest, too. Or perhaps he floated onward and without running-lights, through nighted chambers.

149

"It was held once a year in the Great Hall," the gunslinger went on. "We called it The Hall of Grandfathers. But it was only the Great Hall."

The sound of dripping water came to their ears.

"A courting rite." The gunslinger laughed deprecatingly, and the insensate walls made the sound into a loonlike wheeze. "In the old days, the books say, it was the welcoming of spring. But civilization, you know. . . . "

He trailed off, unable to describe the change inherent in that mechanized noun, the death of the romantic and its sterile, carnal revenant, living only a forced respiration of glitter and ceremony; the geometric steps of courtship during the Easter-night dance at the Great Hall which had replaced the mad scribble of love which he could only intuit dimly — hollow grandeur in the place of mean and sweeping passions which might once have erased souls.

"They made something decadent out of it," the gunslinger said. "A play. A game." In his voice was all the unconscious distaste of the ascetic. His face, had there been stronger light to illumine it, would have shown change — harshness and sorrow. But his essential force had not been cut or diluted. The lack of imagination that still remained in that face was remarkable.

"But the Ball," the gunslinger said. "The Ball . . . "

The boy did not speak.

"There were five crystal chandeliers, heavy glass with electric lights. It was all light, it was an island of light.

"We had sneaked into one of the old balconies, the ones that were supposed to be unsafe. But we were still boys. We were above everything, and we could look down on it. I don't remember that any of us said anything. We only looked, and we looked for hours.

"There was a great stone table where the gunslingers and their women sat, watching the dancers. A few of the gunslingers danced, but only a few. And they were the young ones. The other ones only sat, and it seemed to me they were half embarrassed in all that light, that civilized light. They were revered ones, the feared ones, the guardians, but they seemed like hostlers in that crowd of cavaliers with their soft women. . . .

"There were four circular tables loaded with food, and they turned all the time. The cooks' boys never stopped coming and going from seven until three the next morning. The tables rotated like clocks, and we could smell roast pork, beef, lobster, chickens, baked apples. There were ices and candies. There were great flaming skewers of meat.

"And Marten sat next to my mother and father — I knew them even from so high above — and once she and Marten danced, slowly and revolvingly, and the others cleared the floor for them and clapped when it was over. The gunslingers did not clap, but my father stood slowly and held his hands out to her. And she went, smiling.

"It was a moment of passage, boy. A time such as must be at the Tower itself, when things come together and hold and make power in time. My father had taken control, had been acknowledged and singled out. Marten was the acknowledger; my father was the mover. And his wife my mother, went to him, the connection between them. Betrayer.

"My father was the last lord of light."

The gunslinger looked down at his hands. The boy still said nothing. His face was only thoughtful.

"I remember how they danced," the gunslinger said softly. "My mother and Marten the enchanter. I remember how they danced, revolving slowly together and apart, in the old steps of courtship."

IIe looked at the boy, smiling. "But it meant nothing, you know. Because power had been passed in some way that none of them knew but all understood, and my mother was locked root and rind to the holder and wielder of that power. Was it not so? She went to him when the dance was over, didn't she? And clasped his hand? Did they applaud? Did the hall ring with it as those pansy-boys and their soft ladies applauded and lauded him? Did it? Did it?"

Bitter water dripped distantly in the darkness. The boy said nothing.

"I remember how they danced," the gunslinger said softly. "I remember how they danced. . . . " He looked up at the unseeable stone roof and it seemed for a moment that he might scream at it, rail at it, challenge it blindly — those dumb tonnages of insensible granite that bore their tiny lives in its stone intestine.

"What hand could have held the knife that did my father to his death?"

"I'm tired," the boy said wistfully.

The gunslinger lapsed into silence, and the boy laid over and put one hand between his cheek and the stone. The little flame in front of them guttered. The gunslinger rolled a smoke. It seemed he could see the crystal light still, in the sardonic hall of his memory; hear the shout of accolade, empty in a husked land that stood even then hopeless against a gray ocean of time. The island of light hurt him bitterly, and he wished he had never held witness to it, or to his father's cuckoldry.

He passed smoke between his mouth and nostrils, looking down at the boy. How we make large circles in earth for ourselves, he thought. How long before the daylight again?

He slept.

After the sound of his breathing had become long and steady and regular, the boy opened his eyes and looked at the gunslinger with an expression that was very much like love. The last light of the fire caught in one pupil for a moment and was drowned there. He went to sleep.

The gunslinger had lost most of his time sense in the desert, which was changeless; he lost the rest of it here in these chambers under the mountains, which were lightless. Neither of them had any means of telling time, and the concept of hours became meaningless. In a sense, they stood outside of time. A day might have been a week, or a week a day. They walked, they slept, they ate thinly. Their only companion was the steady thundering rush of the water, drilling its auger path through the stone. They followed it, drank from its flat, mineral-salted depth. At times the gunslinger thought he saw fugitive drifting lights like corpse-lamps beneath its surface, but supposed they were only projections of his brain, which had not forgotten the light. Still, he cautioned the boy not to put his feet in the water.

The range finder in his head took them on steadily.

The path beside the river (for it was a path; smooth, sunken to a slight concavity) led always upward, toward the river's head. At regular intervals they came to curved stone pylons with sunken ringbolts; perhaps once oxen or stage-horses had tethered there. At each was a steel flagon holding an electric torch, but these were all barren of life and light.

During the third period of rest-before-sleep, the boy wandered away a little. The gunslinger could hear small conversation of rattled pebbles as he moved cautiously.

"Careful," he said. "You can't see where you are."

"I'm crawling. It's . . . say!"

"What is it?" The gunslinger half crouched, touching the haft of one gun.

There was a slight pause. The gunslinger strained his eyes uselessly.

"I think it's a railroad," the boy said dubiously.

The gunslinger got up and walked slowly toward the sound of Jake's voice, leading with one foot lightly to test for pitfalls.

"Here." A hand reached out and cat's-pawed the gunslinger's face. The boy was very good in the dark, better than the gunslinger himself. His eyes seemed to dilate until there was no color left in them: the gunslinger saw this as he struck a meager light. There was no fuel in this rock womb, and what they had brought with them was going rapidly to ash. At times the urge to strike a light was well-nigh insatiable.

The boy was standing beside a curved rock wall that was lined with parallel metal staves off into the darkness. Each carried black bulbs that might once have been conductors of electricity. And beside and below, set only inches off the stone floor, were tracks of bright metal. What might have run on those tracks at one time? The gunslinger could only imagine black electric bullets, flying through this forever night with affrighted searchlight eyes going before. He had never heard of such things. But there were skeletons in the world, just as there were demons. He had once come upon a hermit who had gained a quasi-religious power over a miserable flock of kine-keepers by possession of an ancient gasoline pump. The hermit crouched beside it, one arm wrapped possessively around it, and preached wild, guttering, sullen sermons. He occasionally placed the still-bright steel nozzle, which was attached to a rotted rubber hose, between his legs. On the pump, in perfectly legible (although rust-clotted) letters, was a legend of unknown meaning: *AMOCO. Lead Free.* Amoco had become the totem of a thundergod, and they had worshipped Him with the half-mad slaughter of sheep.

Hulks, the gunslinger thought. Only meaningless hulks in sands that once were seas.

And now a railroad.

"We'll follow it," he said.

The boy said nothing.

The gunslinger extinguished the light and they slept. When the gunslinger awoke the boy was up before him, sitting on one of the rails and watching him sightlessly in the dark.

They followed the rails like blindmen, the gunslinger leading, the boy following. They slipped their feet along one rail always, also like blindmen. The steady rush of the river off to the right was their companion. They did not speak, and this went on for three periods of waking. The gunslinger felt no urge to think coherently, or to plan. His sleep was dreamless.

During the fourth period of waking and walking, they literally stumbled on a handcar.

The gunslinger ran into it chest-high, and the boy, walking on the other side, struck his forehead and went down with a cry.

The gunslinger made a light immediately. "Are you all right?" The words sounded sharp, almost waspish, and he winced at them.

"Yes." The boy was holding his head gingerly. He shook it once to make sure he had told the truth. They turned to look at what they had run into.

It was a flat square of metal that sat mutely on the tracks. There was a see-saw handle in the center of the square. The gunslinger had no immediate sense of it, but the boy knew immediately.

"It's a handcar."

"What?"

"Handcar," the boy said impatiently, "like in the old movies. Look."

He pulled himself up and went to the handle. He managed to push it down, but it was necessary to hang all his weight on the handle. He grunted briefly. The handcar moved a foot, with silent timelessness, on the rails.

"It works a little hard," the boy said, as if apologizing for it.

The gunslinger pulled himself up and pushed the handle down. The handcar moved forward obediently, then stopped. he could feel a drive-shaft turn beneath his feet. The operation pleased him — it was the first old machine other than the pump at the way station that he had seen in years which still worked well — but it disquieted him, too. It would take them to their destination that much quicker. The curse-kiss again, he thought, and knew the man in black had meant them to find this, too.

"Neat, huh?" The boy said, and his voice was full of loathing.

"What are movies?" The gunslinger asked again.

Jake still did not answer and they stood in a black silence, like in a tomb where life had fled. The gunslinger could hear his organs at work inside his body and the boy's respiration. That was all.

"You stand on one side. I stand on the other side," Jake said. "You'll have to push by yourself until it gets rolling good. Then I can help. First you push, then I push. We'll go right along. Get it?"

"I get it," the gunslinger said. His hands were in helpless, despairing fists.

"But you'll have to push by yourself until it gets rolling good," the boy repeated, looking at him.

The gunslinger had a sudden vivid picture of the Great Hall a year after the spring Ball, in the shattered, hulked shards of revolt, civil strife, and invasion. It was followed with the memory of Allie, the woman from Tull with the scar, pushed and pulled by the bullets that were killing her in reflex. It was followed by Jamie's face, blue in death, by

Susan's, twisted and weeping. All my old friends, the gunslinger thought, and smiled hideously.

"I'll push," the gunslinger said.

He began to push.

They rolled on through the dark, faster now, no longer
having to feel their way. Once the awkwardness of a buried
age had been run off the handcar, it went smoothly. The
boy tried to do his share, and the gunslinger allowed him
small shifts — but mostly he pumped by himself, in large
and chest-stretching rises and fallings. The river was their
companion, sometimes closer on their right, sometimes
further away. Once it took on huge and thunderous hollow-
ness, as if passing through a prehistoric cathedral narthex.
Once the sound of it disappeared almost altogether.

The speed and the made wind against their faces seemed
to take the place of sight and to put them once again in a
frame of time and reference. The gunslinger estimated they
were making anywhere from ten to fifteen miles an hour,
always on a shallow, almost imperceptible uphill grade that
wore him out deceptively. When they stopped he slept like
the stone itself. Their food was almost gone again. Neither
of them worried about it.

For the gunslinger, the tenseness of a coming climax
was as imperceivable but as real and as accretive as the
fatigue of propelling the handcar. They were close to the
end of the beginning. He felt like a performer placed on
center stage minutes before the rise of the curtain; settled
in position with his first line held in his mind, he heard the
unseen audience rattling programs and settling in seats. He
lived with a tight, tidy ball of unholy anticipation in his
belly and welcomed the exercise that let him sleep.

The boy spoke less and less; but at their stopping place
one sleep-period before they were attacked by the Slow

Mutants, he asked the gunslinger almost shyly about his coming of age.

The gunslinger had been leaning against the handle, a cigarette from his dwindling supply of tobacco clamped in his mouth. He had been on the verge of his usual unthinking sleep when the boy asked his question.

"Why would you want to know that?" He asked.

The boy's voice was curiously stubborn, as if hiding embarrassment. "I just do." And after a pause, he added: "I always wondered about growing up. It's mostly lies."

"It wasn't growing up," the gunslinger said. "I never grew up all at once. I did it one place and another along the way. I saw a man hung once. That was part of it, though I didn't know it then. I left a girl in a place called King's Town twelve years ago. That was another part. I never knew any of the parts when they happened. Only later I knew that."

He realized with some unease that he was avoiding.

"I suppose the coming of age was part, too," he said, almost grudgingly. "It was formal. Almost stylized; like a dance." He laughed unpleasantly. "Like love.

"Love and dying have been my life."

The boy said nothing.

"It was necessary to prove one's self in battle," the gunslinger began.

Summer and hot.

August had come to the land like a vampire lover, killing the land and the crops of the tenant farmers, turning the fields of the castle-city white and sterile. In the west, some miles distant and near the borders that were the end of the civilized world, fighting had already begun. All reports were bad, and all of them palled before the heat that rested over this place of the center. Cattle lolled empty-eyed in the pens of the stockyards. Pigs grunted list-lessly, unmindful of knives whetted for the coming fall. People whined about taxes and conscription, as they always have; but there was an emptiness beneath the apathetic passion play of politics. The center had frayed like a rag rug that had been washed and walked on and shaken and hung and dried. The lines and nets of mesh which held the last jewel at the breast of the world were unraveling. Things were not holding together. The earth drew in its breath in the summer of the coming eclipse.

The boy idled along the upper corridor of this stone place which was home, sensing these things, not under-standing. He was also empty and dangerous.

It had been three years since the hanging of the cook who had always been able to find snacks for hungry boys, and he had filled out. Now, dressed only in faded denim pants, fourteen years old, he had already come to the wid-ened chest-span and lengthening legs that would charac-terize his manhood. He was still unbedded, but two of the younger slatterns of a West-Town merchant had cast eyes on him. He had felt a response and felt it more strongly now. Even in the coolness of the passage, he felt sweat on his body.

Ahead were his mother's apartments and he approached them incuriously, meaning only to pass them and go up-ward to the roof, where a thin breeze and the pleasure of his hand awaited.

He had passed the door when a voice called him: "You. Boy."

It was Marten, the enchanter. He was dressed with a suspicious, upsetting casualness — black whipcord trousers almost as tight as leotards, and a white shirt open halfway down his chest. His hair was tousled.

The boy looked at him silently.

"Come in, come in! Don't stand in the hall! Your mother wants to speak to you." He was smiling with his mouth, but the lines of his face held a deeper, more sardonic humor. Beneath that there was only coldness.

But his mother did not seem to want to see him. She sat in the low-backed chair by the large window in the central parlor of her apartments, the one which overlooked the hot blank stone of the central courtyard. She was dressed in a loose, informal gown and looked at the boy only once — a quick, glinting rueful smile, like autumn sun on stream water. During the rest of the interview she studied her hands.

He saw her seldom now, and the phantom of cradle songs had almost faded from his brain. But she was a beloved stranger. He felt an amorphous fear, and an uncoalesced hatred for Marten, his father's right-hand man (or was it the other way around?), was born.

And, of course, there had already been some back-street talk — talk which he honestly thought he hadn't heard.

"Are you well?" She asked him softly, studying her hands. Marten stood beside her, a heavy, disturbing hand near the juncture of her white shoulder and white neck, smiling on them both. His brown eyes were dark to the point of blackness with smiling.

"Yes," he said.

"Your studies go well?"

"I'm trying," he said. They both knew he was not flashingly intelligent like Cuthbert, or even quick, like Jamie. He was a plodder and a bludgeoner.

"And David?" She knew his affection for the hawk.

The boy looked up at Marten, still smiling paternally down on all this. "Past his prime."

His mother seemed to wince; for a moment Marten's face seemed to darken, his grip on her shoulder tighten.

Then she looked out into the hot whiteness of the day, and all was as it had been.

It's a charade, he thought. A game. Who is playing with whom?

"You have a scar on your forehead," Marten said, still smiling. "Are you going to be a fighter like your father or are you just slow?"

This time she did wince.

"Both," the boy said. He looked steadily at Marten and smiled painfully. Even in here, it was very hot.

Marten stopped smiling abruptly. "You can go to the roof now, boy. I believe you have business there."

But Marten had misunderstood, underestimated. They had been speaking in the low tongue, a parody of informality. But now the boy flashed into High Speech:

"My mother has not yet dismissed me, bondsman!"

Marten's face twisted as if quirt-lashed. The boy heard his mother's dreadful, woeful gasp. She spoke his name.

But the painful smile remained intact on the boy's face and he stepped forward. "Will you give me a sign of fealty, bondsman? In the name of my father whom you serve?"

Marten stared at him, rankly unbelieving.

"Go," Marten said gently. "Go and find your hand."

Smiling, the boy went.

As he closed the door and went back the way he came, he heard his mother wail. It was a banshee sound.

Then he heard Marten's laugh.

The boy continued to smile as he went to his test.

Jamie had come from the shop-wives, and when he saw the boy crossing the exercise yard, he ran to tell Roland the latest gossips of bloodshed and revolt to the west. But he fell aside, the words all unspoken. They had known each other since the time of infancy, and as boys they had dared

each other, cuffed each other, and made a thousand explor
ations of the walls within which they had both been birthed.

The boy strode past him, staring without seeing, grinning his painful grin. He was walking toward Cort's cottage, where the shades were drawn to ward off the savage
afternoon heat. Cort napped in the afternoon so that he could
enjoy his evening tomcat forays into the mazed and filthy
brothels of the lower town to the fullest extent.

Jamie knew in a flash of intuition, knew what was to
come, and in his fear and ecstasy he was torn between following Roland and going after the others.

Then his hypnotism was broken and he ran toward the
main buildings, screaming. "Cuthbert! Allen! Thomas!" His
screams sounded puny and thin in the heat. They had
known, all of them, in that invisible way boys have, that the
boy would be the first of them to try the line. But this was
too soon.

The hideous grin on Roland's face galvanized him
as no news of wars, revolts, and witchcrafts could have done.
This was more than words from a toothless mouth given
over fly-specked heads of lettuce.

Roland walked to the cottage of his teacher and kicked
the door open. It slammed backward, hit the plain rough
plaster of the wall and rebounded.

He had never been here before. The entrance opened
on an austere kitchen that was cool and brown. A table. Two
straight chairs. Two cabinets. A faded linoleum floor,
tracked in black paths from the cooler set in the floor to the
counter where knives hung, to the table.

A public man's privacy here. The last faded sobriety of
a violent midnight carouser who had loved the boys of three
generations roughly, and made some of them into gunslingers.

"Cort!"

He kicked the table, sending it across the room and into the counter. Knives from the wall rack fell in twinkling jackstraws.

There was thick stirring in the other room, a half-sleep clearing of the throat. The boy did not enter, knowing it was sham, knowing that Cort had awakened immediately in the cottage's other room and stood with one glittering eye beside the door, waiting to break the intruder's unwary neck.

"Cort, I want you, bondsman!"

Now he spoke the High Speech, and Cort swung the door open. He was dressed only in thin underwear shorts, a squat man with bow legs, runneled with scars from top to toe, thick with twists of muscle. There was a round, bulging belly. The boy knew from experience that it was spring steel. The one good eye glared at him from the bashed and dented hairless head.

The boy saluted formally. "Teach me no more, bondsman. Today I teach you."

"You are early, puler," he said casually, but he also spoke the High Speech. "Five years early, I should judge. I will ask only once. Will you renege?"

The boy only smiled his hideous, painful smile. For Cort, who had seen the smile on a score of bloodied, scarlet-skied fields of honor and dishonor, it was answer enough — perhaps the only answer he would have believed.

"It's too bad," the teacher said absently. "You have been a most promising pupil — the best in two dozen years, I should say. It will be sad to see you broken and set upon a blind path. But the world has moved on. Bad times are on horseback."

The boy still did not speak (and would have been incapable of any coherent explanation, had it been required), but for the first time the awful smile softened a little.

"Still, there is the line of blood," Cort said somberly, "revolt and witchcraft to the west or no. I am your bondsman, boy. I recognize your command and bow to it now — if never again — with my heart."

And Cort, who had cuffed him, kicked him, bled him, cursed him, made mock of him and called him the very eye of syphilis, bent to one knee and bowed his head.

The boy touched the leathery, vulnerable flesh of his neck with wonder, "Rise, bondsman. In love."

Cort stood slowly, and there might have been pain behind the impassive mask of his reamed features. "This is waste. Renege, boy. I break my own oath. Renege, and wait!"

The boy said nothing.

"Very well." Cort's voice became dry and businesslike. "One hour. And the weapon of your choice."

"You will bring your stick?"

"I always have."

"How many sticks have been taken from you, Cort?" Which was tantamount to asking: How many boys have entered the square yard beyond the Great Hall and returned as gunslinger apprentices?

"No stick will be taken from me today," Cort said slowly. "I regret it. There is only the once, boy. The penalty for overeagerness is the same as the penalty for unworthiness. Can you not wait?"

The boy recalled Marten standing over him, tall as mountains. "No."

"Very well. What weapon do you choose?"

The boy said nothing.

Cort's smile showed a jagged ring of teeth. "Wise enough to begin. In an hour. You realize you will in all probability never see the others, or your father, or this place again?"

"I know what exile means," he said softly.

"Go now."

The boy went, without looking back.

The cellar of the barn was spuriously cool, dank, smelling of cobwebs and earthwater. It was lit from the ubiquitous sun, but felt none of the day's heat; the boy kept the hawk here and the bird seemed comfortable enough.

David was old, now, and no longer hunted the sky. His feathers had lost the radiant animal brightness of three years ago, but the eyes were still as piercing and motionless as ever. You cannot friend a hawk, they said, unless you are a hawk yourself, alone and only a sojourner in the land, without friends or the need of them. The hawk pays no coinage to morals.

David was an old hawk now. The boy hoped (or was he too unimaginative to hope? Did he only know?) that he himself was a young one.

"Hai," he said softly and extended his arm to the tethered perch.

The hawk stepped onto the boy's arm and stood motionless, unhooded. With his other hand the boy reached into his pocket and fished out a bit of dried jerky. The hawk snapped it deftly from between his fingers and made it disappear.

The boy began to stroke David very carefully. Cort most probably would not have believed it if he had seen it, but Cort did not believe the boy's time had come, either.

"I think you die today," he said, continuing to stroke. "I think you will be made sacrifice, like all those little birds we trained you on. Do you remember? No? It doesn't matter. After today, I am the hawk."

David stood on his arm, silent and unblinking, indifferent to his life or death.

"You are old," the boy said reflectively. "And perhaps not my friend. Even a year ago you would have had my eyes instead of that little string of meat, isn't it so? Cort would laugh. But if we get close enough . . . which is it, bird? Age or friendship?"

David did not say.

The boy hooded him and found the jesses, which were looped at the end of David's perch. They left the barn.

The yard behind the Great Hall was not really a yard at all, but only a green corridor whose walls were formed by tangled, thick-grown hedges. It had been used for the rite of coming of age since time out of mind, long before Cort and his predecessor, who had died of a stab-wound from an overzealous hand in this place. Many boys had left the corridor from the east end, where the teacher always entered, as men. The east end faced the Great Hall and all the civilization and intrigue of the lighted world. Many more had slunk away, beaten and bloody, from the west end, where the boys always entered, as boys forever. The west end faced the mountains and the hut-dwellers; beyond that, the tangled barbarian forests; and beyond that the desert. The boy who became a man progressed from darkness and unlearning to light and responsibility. The boy who was beaten could only retreat, forever and forever. The hallway was as smooth and green as a gaming field. It was exactly fifty yards long.

Each end was usually clogged with tense spectators and relatives, for the ritual was usually forecast with great accuracy — eighteen was the most common age (those who had not made their test by the age of twenty-five usually slipped into obscurity as freeholders, unable to face the brutal all-or-nothing fact of the field and the test). But on

this day there were none but Jamie, Cuthbert, Allen, and
Thomas. They clustered at the boy's end, gape-mouthed
and frankly terrified.

"Your weapon, stupid!" Cuthbert hissed, in agony.
"You forgot your weapon!"

"I have it," the boy said distantly. Dimly he wondered
if the news of this had reached yet to the central buildings,
to his mother — and Marten. His father was on a hunt, not
due back for weeks. In this he felt a sense of shame, for he
felt that in his father he would have found understanding,
if not approval. "Has Cort come?"

"Cort is here." The voice came from the far end of the
corridor, and Cort stepped into view, dressed in a short
singlet. A heavy leather band encircled his forehead to
keep sweat from his eyes. He held an ironwood stick in one
hand, sharp on one end, heavily blunted and spatulate on
the other. He began the litany which all of them, chosen by
the blind blood of their fathers, had known since early
childhood, learned against the day when they would, perchance, become men.

"Have you come here for a serious purpose, boy?"

"I have come for a serious purpose, teacher."

"Have you come as an outcast from your father's
house?"

"I have so come, teacher." And would remain outcast
until he had bested Cort. If Cort bested him, he would remain outcast forever.

"Have you come with your chosen weapon?"

"I have so come, teacher."

"What is your weapon?" This was the teacher's advantage, his chance to adjust his plan of battle to the sling
or the spear or the net.

"My weapon is David, teacher."

Cort halted only briefly.

"So then have you at me, boy?"

"I do."

"Be swift, then."

And Cort advanced into the corridor, switching his pike from one hand to the other. The boys sighed flutteringly, like birds, as their compatriot stepped to meet him.

My weapon is David, teacher.

Did Cort remember? Had he fully understood? If so, perhaps it was all lost. It turned on surprise — and on whatever stuff the hawk had left in him. Would he only sit, disinterested, on the boy's arm, while Cort struck him brainless with the ironwood? Or seek the high, hot sky?

They drew close together, and the boy loosened the hawk's hood with nerveless fingers. It dropped to the green grass, and the boy halted in his tracks. He saw Cort's eyes drop to the bird and widen with surprise and slow-dawning comprehension.

Now, then.

"At him!" The boy cried and raised his arm.

And David flew like a silent brown bullet, stubby wings pumping once, twice, three times, before crashing into Cort's face, talons and beak searching.

"Hai! Roland!" Cuthbert screamed deliriously.

Cort staggered backwards, off balance. The ironwood staff rose and beat futilely at the air about his head. The hawk was an undulating, blurred bundle of feathers.

The boy arrowed forward, his hand held out in a straight wedge, his elbow locked.

Still, Cort was almost too quick for him. The bird had covered ninety percent of his vision, but the ironwood came up again, spatulate end forward, and Cort coldbloodedly performed the only action that could turn events at that point. He beat his own face three times, biceps flexing mercilessly.

David fell away, broken and twisted. One wing flapped at the ground frantically. His cold, predator's eyes stared fiercely into the teacher's bloody, streaming face. Cort's bad eye now bulged blindly from its socket.

The boy delivered a kick to Cort's temple, connecting solidly. It should have ended it; his leg had been numbed by Cort's only blow, but it still should have ended it. It did not. For a moment Cort's face went slack, and then he lunged, grabbing for the boy's foot.

The boy skipped back and tripped over his own feet. He went down asprawl. He heard, from far away the sound of Jamie's scream.

Cort was up, ready to fall on him and finish it. He had lost his advantage. For a moment they looked at each other, the teacher standing over the pupil, with gouts of blood pouring from the left side of his face, the bad eye now closed except for a thin slit of white. There would be no brothels for Cort this night.

Something ripped jaggedly at the boy's hand. It was the hawk, David, tearing blindly. Both wings were broken. It was incredible that he still lived.

The boy grabbed him like a stone, unmindful of the jabbing, diving beak that was taking the flesh from his wrist in ribbons. As Cort flew at him, all spread-eagled, the boy threw the hawk upward.

"Hai! David! Kill!"

Then Cort blotted out the sun and came down atop of him.

The bird was smashed between them, and the boy felt a calloused thumb probe for the socket of his eye. He turned it, at the same time bringing up the slab of his thigh to block Cort's crotch-seeking knee. His own hand flailed against the tree of Cort's neck in three hard chops. It was like hitting ribbed stone.

Then Cort made a thick grunting. His body shuddered. Faintly, the boy saw one hand flailing for the dropped stick, and with a jackknifing lunge, he kicked it out of reach. David had hooked one talon into Cort's right ear. The other battered mercilessly at the teacher's cheek, making it a ruin. Warm blood splattered the boy's face, smelling of sheared copper.

Cort's fist struck the bird once, breaking it's back. Again, and the neck snapped away at a crooked angle. And still the talon clutched. There was no ear now; only a red hole tunneled into the side of Cort's skull. The third blow sent the bird flying, clearing Cort's face.

The boy brought the edge of his hand across the bridge of Cort's nose, breaking the thin bone. Blood sprayed.

Cort's grasping, unseeing hand ripped at the boy's buttocks and Roland rolled away blindly, finding Cort's stick, rising to his knees.

Cort came to his own knees, grinning. His face was curtained with gore. The one seeing eye rolled madly in its socket. The nose was smashed over to a haunted, leaning angle. Both cheeks hung in flaps.

The boy held his stick like a baseball player waiting for the pitch.

Cort double-feinted, then came directly at him.

The boy was ready. The ironwood swung in a flat arc, striking Cort's skull with a dull thudding noise. Cort fell on his side, looking at the boy with a lazy unseeing expression. A tiny trickle of spit came from his mouth.

"Yield or die," the boy said. His mouth was filled with wet cotton.

And Cort smiled. Nearly all consciousness was gone, and he would remain tended in his cottage for a week afterward, wrapped in the blackness of coma, but now he held on with all the strength of his pitiless, shadowless life.

"I yield, gunslinger. I yield smiling."

Cort's clear eye closed.

The gunslinger shook him gently, but with persistence. The others were around him now, their hands trembling to thump his back and hoist him to their shoulders; but they held back, afraid, sensing a new gulf. Yet it was not as strange as it could have been, because there had always been a gulf between this one and the rest.

Cort's eye fluttered open again, weakly.

"The key," the gunslinger said. "My birthright, teacher. I need it."

His birthright was the guns — not the heavy ones of his father, weighted with sandalwood — but guns, all the same. Forbidden to all but a few. The ultimate, the final weapon. In the heavy vault under the barracks where he by ancient law was now required to abide, away from his mother's breast, hung his apprentice weapons, heavy cumbersome things of steel and nickel. Yet they had seen his father through his apprenticeship, and his father now ruled — at least in name.

"Is it so fearsome, then?" Cort muttered, as if in his sleep. "So pressing? I feared so. And yet you won."

"The key."

"The hawk . . . a fine ploy. A fine weapon. How long did it take you to train the bastard?"

"I never trained David. I friended him. The key."

"Under my belt, gunslinger." The eye closed again.

The gunslinger reached under Cort's belt, feeling the heavy press of his belly, the huge muscles there now slack and asleep. The key was on a brass ring. He clutched it in his hand, restraining the mad urge to thrust it up to the sky in a salutation of victory.

He got to his feet and was finally turning to the others

when Cort's hand fumbled for his foot. For a moment the gunslinger feared some last attack and tensed, but Cort only looked up at him and beckoned with one crusted finger.

"I'm going to sleep now," Cort whispered calmly. "Perhaps forever, I don't know. I teach you no more, gunslinger. You have surpassed me, and two years younger than your father, who was the youngest. But let me counsel."

"What?" Impatiently.

"Wait."

"Huh?" The word was startled out of him.

"Let the word and the legend go before you. There are those who will carry both." His eyes flicked over the gunslinger's shoulder. "Fools, perchance. Let the word go before you. Let your shadow grow. Let it grow hair on its face. Let it become dark." He smiled grotesquely. "Given time, words may even enchant an enchanter. Do you take my meaning, gunslinger?"

"Yes."

"Will you take my last counsel?"

The gunslinger rocked back on his heels, a hunkered, thinking posture that foreshadowed the man. He looked at the sky. It was deepening, purpling. The heat of the day was failing and thunderheads in the west foretold rain. Lightning tines jabbed the placid flank of the rising foothills miles distant. Beyond that, the mountains. Beyond that, the rising fountains of blood and unreason. He was tired, tired into his bones and beyond.

He looked back at Cort. "I will bury my hawk tonight, teacher. And later go into lower town to inform those in the brothels that will wonder about you."

Cort's lips parted in a pained smile. And then he slept.

The gunslinger got to his feet and turned to the others. "Make a litter and take him to his house. Then bring a nurse. No, two nurses. Okay?"

They still watched him, caught in a bated moment that was not yet able to be broken. They still looked for a corona of fire, or a werewolf change of features.

"Two nurses," the gunslinger repeated, and then smiled. They smiled.

"You god-damned horse drover!" Cuthbert suddenly yelled, grinning. "You haven't left enough meat for the rest of us to pick off the bone!"

"The world won't move on tomorrow," the gunslinger said, quoting the old adage with a smile. "Allen, you butter-ass. Move your freight."

Allen set about making the litter; Thomas and Jamie went together to the main hall and the infirmary.

The gunslinger and Cuthbert looked at each other. They had always been the closest — or as close as they could be under the particular shades of their characters. There was a speculative, open light in Cuthbert's eyes, and the gunslinger controlled only with great difficulty the need to tell him not to call for the test for a year or even eighteen months, lest he go west. But they had been through a great deal together, and the gunslinger did not feel he could risk it without an expression that might be taken for patronization. I've begun to scheme, he thought, and was a little dismayed. Then he thought of Marten, of his mother, and he smiled a deceiver's smile at his friend.

I am to be the first, he thought, knowing it for the first time, although he had thought of it (in a bemused way) many times before. I am to be first.

"Let's go," he said.

"With pleasure, gunslinger."

They left by the east end of the hedge-bordered corridor; Thomas and Jamie were returning with the nurses already. They looked like ghosts in their heavy white robes, crossed at the breast with red.

"Shall I help you with the hawk?" Cuthbert asked.

"Yes," the gunslinger said.

And later, when darkness had come and the rushing thundershowers with it; while huge, phantom caissons rolled across the sky and lightning washed the crooked streets of the lower town in blue fire; while horses stood at hitching rails with their heads down and their tails drooping, the gunslinger took a woman and lay with her.

It was quick and good. When it was over and they lay side by side without speaking, it began to hail with a brief, rattling ferocity. Downstairs and far away, someone was playing *Hey Jude* ragtime. The gunslinger's mind turned reflectively inward. It was in that hail-splattered silence, just before sleep overtook him, that he first thought that he might also be the last.

The gunslinger did not, of course, tell the boy all of this, but perhaps most of it had come through anyway. He had already realized that this was an extremely perceptive boy, not so different from Cuthbert, or even Jamie.

"You asleep?" the gunslinger asked.

"No."

"Did you understand what I told you?"

"Understand it?" The boy asked, with cautious scorn. "Understand it? Are you kidding?"

"No." But the gunslinger felt defensive. He had never told anyone about his coming of age before, because he felt ambivalent about it. Of course, the hawk had been a perfectly acceptable weapon, yet it had been a trick, too. And a betrayal. The first of many: *Am I readying to throw this boy at the man in black?*

"I understood it," the boy said. "It was a game, wasn't it? Do grown men always have to play games? Does everything have to be an excuse for another kind of game? Do any men grow up or do they only come of age?"

"You don't know everything," the gunslinger said, trying to hold his slow anger.

"No. But I know what I am to you."

"And what is that?" The gunslinger asked tightly.

"A poker chip."

The gunslinger felt an urge to find a rock and brain the boy. Instead, he held his tongue.

"Go to sleep," he said. "Boys need their sleep."

And in his mind he heard Marten's echo: *Go and find your hand.*

He sat stiffly in the darkness, stunned with horror and terrified (for the first time in his existence; of anything) of the self-loathing that might come.

During the next period of waking, the railway angled closer to the underground river, and they came upon the Slow Mutants.

Jake saw the first one and screamed aloud.

The gunslinger's head, which had been fixed straight forward as he pumped the handcar, jerked to the right. There was a rotten jack-o-lantern greenness below and away from them, circular and pulsating faintly. For the first time he became aware of odor — faint, unpleasant, wet.

The greenness was a face, and the face was abnormal. Above the flattened nose was an insectile node of eyes, looking at them expressionlessly. The gunslinger felt an atavistic crawl in his intestines and privates. He stepped up the rhythm of arms and handcar handle slightly.

The glowing face faded.

"What was it?" the boy asked, crawling. "What — " The words stopped dumb in his throat as they came up upon and passed a group of three faintly glowing forms, standing between the rails and the invisible river, watching them, motionless.

"They're Slow Mutants," the gunslinger said. "I don't

think they'll bother us. They're probably just as frightened of us as we are of — "

One of the forms broke free and shambled toward them, glowing and changing. The face was that of a starving idiot. The faint naked body had been transformed into a knotted mess of tentacular limbs with suckers.

The boy screamed again and crowded against the gunslinger's leg like an affrighted dog.

One of the tentacles pawed across the flat platform of the handcar. It reeked of the wet and the dark and of strangeness. The gunslinger let loose of the handle and drew. He put a bullet through the forehead of the starving idiot face. It fell away, its faint swamp-fire glow fading, an eclipsed moon. The gunflash lay bright and branded on their dark retinas, fading only reluctantly. The smell of expended powder was hot and savage and alien in this buried place.

There were others, more of them. None moved against them overtly, but they were closing in on the tracks, a silent, hideous party of rubberneckers.

"You may have to pump for me," the gunslinger said. "Can you?"

"Yes."

"Then be ready."

The boy stood close to him, his body poised. His eyes took in the Slow Mutants only as they passed, not traversing, not seeing more than they had to. The boy assumed a psychic bulge of terror, as if his very id had somehow sprung out through his pores to form a telepathic shield.

The gunslinger pumped steadily but did not increase his speed. The Slow Mutants could smell their terror, he knew that, but he doubted if terror would be enough for them. He and the boy were, after all, creatures of the light, and whole. How they must hate us, he thought, and wondered if they had hated the man in black in the same way.

He thought not, or perhaps he had passed among them and through their pitiful hive colony unknown, only the shadow of a dark wing.

The boy made a noise in his throat and the gunslinger turned his head almost casually. Four of them were charging the handcar in a stumbling way — one of them in the process of finding a handgrip.

The gunslinger let go of the handle and drew again, with the same sleepy casual motion. He shot the lead mutant in the head. The mutant made a sighing, sobbing noise and began to grin. Its hands were limp and fishlike, dead; the fingers clove to one another like the fingers of a glove long immersed in drying mud. One of these corpse-hands found the boy's foot and began to pull.

The boy shrieked aloud in the granite womb.

The gunslinger shot the mutant in the chest. It began to slobber through the grin. Jake was going off the side. The gunslinger caught one of his arms and was almost pulled off balance himself. The thing was amazingly strong. The gunslinger put another bullet in the mutant's head. One eye went out like a candle. Still it pulled. They engaged in a silent tug of war for Jake's jerking, wriggling body. They yanked on him like a wishbone.

The handcar was slowing down. The others began to close in — the lame, the halt, the blind. Perhaps they only looked for a Jesus to heal them, to raise them Lazarus-like from the darkness.

It's the end for the boy, the gunslinger thought with perfect coldness. This is the end he meant. Let go and pump or hold on and be buried. The end for the boy.

He gave a tremendous yank on the boy's arm and shot the mutant in the belly. For one frozen moment its grip grew even tighter and Jake began to slide off the edge again. Then the dead mud-hands loosened, and the Slow Mutie

fell on its face between the tracks behind the slowing handcar, still grinning.

"I thought you'd leave me," the boy was sobbing. "I
thought . . . I thought. . . . "

"Hold onto my belt," the gunslinger said. "Hold on
just as tight as you can."

The hand worked into his belt and clutched there; the
boy was breathing in great convulsive, silent gasps.

The gunslinger began to pump steadily again, and the
handcar picked up speed. The Slow Mutants fell back a step
and watched them go with faces hardly human (or patheti-
cally so), faces that generated the weak phosphorescence
common to those weird deep-sea fishes that live under incredible black pressure, faces that held no anger or hate on
their senseless orbs, but only what seemed to be a semicon-
scious, idiot regret.

"They're thinning," the gunslinger said. The drawn-
up muscles of his lower belly and privates relaxed the smallest bit. "They're — "

The Slow Mutants had put rocks across the track. The
way was blocked. It had been a quick, poor job, perhaps the
work of only a minute to clear, but they were stopped. And
someone would have to get down and move them. The boy
moaned and shuddered closer to the gunslinger. The gunslinger let go of the handle and the handcar coasted noise-
lessly to the rocks, where it thumped to rest.

The Slow Mutants began to close in again, almost casually, almost as if they had been passing by, lost in a dream
of darkness, and had found someone of whom to ask directions. A street-corner congregation of the damned beneath the ancient rock.

"Are they going to get us?" The boy asked calmly.

"No. Be quiet a second."

He looked at the rocks. The mutants were weak, of

course, and had not been able to drag any of the boulders to block their way. Only small rocks. Only enough to stop them, to make someone get down.

"Get down," the gunslinger said. "You'll have to move them. I'll cover you."

"No," the boy whispered. "Please."

"I can't give you a gun and I can't move the rocks and shoot too. You have to get down."

Jake's eyes rolled terribly; for a moment his body shuddered in tune with the turnings of his mind, and then he wriggled over the side and began to throw rocks to the right and the left madly, not looking.

The gunslinger drew and waited.

Two of them, lurching rather than walking, went for the boy with arms like dough. The guns did their work, stitching the darkness with red-white lances of light that pushed needles of pain into the gunslinger's eyes. The boy screamed and continued to throw away rocks. Witch-glow leaped and danced. Hard to see, now, that was the worst. Everything had gone to shadows.

One of them, glowing hardly at all, suddenly reached for the boy with rubber boogeyman arms. Eyes that ate up half the mutie's head rolled wetly.

Jake screamed again and turned to struggle.

The gunslinger fired without allowing himself to think, before his spotty vision could betray his hands into a terrible quiver; the two heads were only inches apart. It was the mutie who fell, slitheringly.

Jake threw rocks wildly. The mutants milled just outside the invisible line of trespass, closing a little at a time, now very close. Others had caught up, swelling their number.

"All right," the gunslinger said. "Get on. Quick."

When the boy moved, the mutants came at them. Jake

was over the side and scrambling to his feet; the gunslinger was already pumping again, all out. Both guns were holstered now. They must run.

Strange hands slapped the metal plane of the car's surface. The boy was holding his belt with both hands now, his face pressed tightly into the small of the gunslinger's back.

A group of them ran onto the tracks, their faces full of that mindless, casual anticipation. The gunslinger was pumped full of adrenalin; the car was flying along the tracks into the darkness. They struck the four or five pitiful hulks full force. They flew like rotten bananas struck from the stem.

On and on, into the soundless, flying, banshee darkness.

After an age, the boy raised his face into the made wind, dreading and yet needing to know. The ghost of gun-flashes still lingered on his retinas. There was nothing to see but the darkness and nothing to hear but the rumble of the river.

"They're gone," the boy said, suddenly fearing an end to the tracks in the darkness, and the wounding crash as they jumped the rails and plunged to twisted ruin. He had ridden in cars; once his humorless father had driven at ninety on the New Jersey Turnpike and had been stopped. But he had never ridden like this, with the wind and the blindness and the terrors behind and ahead, with the sound of the river like a chuckling voice — the voice of the man in black. The gunslinger's arms were pistons in a lunatic human factory.

"They're gone," the boy said timidly, the words ripped from his mouth by the wind. "You can slow down now. We left them behind."

But the gunslinger did not hear. They careened onward into the strange dark.

They went on three periods of waking and sleeping without incident.

During the fourth period of waking (halfway through? three-quarters? they didn't know — only that they weren't tired enough yet to stop) there was a sharp thump beneath them, the handcar swayed, and their bodies immediately leaned to the right with gravity as the rails took a gradual turn to the left.

There was a light ahead — a glow so faint and alien that it seemed at first to be a totally new element, neither earth, air, fire, or water. It had no color and could only be discerned by the fact that they had regained their hands and faces in a dimension beyond that of touch. Their eyes had become so light-sensitive that they noticed the glow over five miles before they approached it.

"The end," the boy said tightly. "It's the end."

"No." The gunslinger spoke with odd assurance. "It isn't."

And it was not. They reached light but not day.

As they approached the source of the glow, they saw for the first time that the rock wall to the left had fallen away and their tracks had been joined by others which crossed in a complex spiderweb. The light laid them in burnished vectors. On some of them there were dark boxcars, passenger coaches, a stage that had been adapted to rails. They made the gunslinger nervous, like ghost galleons trapped in an underground Sargasso.

The light grew stronger, hurting their eyes a little, but growing slowly enough to allow them to adapt. They came from dark to light like divers coming up from deep fathoms in slow stages.

Ahead, drawing nearer, was a huge hangar stretching up into the dark. Cut into it, showing yellow squares of light, were a series of perhaps twenty-four entranceways, growing from the size of toy windows to a height of twenty feet as they drew closer. They passed inside through one of the middle ways. Written above were a series of characters, in various languages, the gunslinger presumed. He was astounded to find that he could read the last one; it was an ancient root of the High Speech itself and said:

TRACK 10 TO SURFACE AND POINTS WEST

The light inside was brighter; the tracks met and merged through a series of switchings. Here some of the traffic lanterns still worked, flashing eternal reds and greens and ambers.

They rolled between rising stone piers caked black with the passage of thousands of vehicles, and then they were in some kind of central terminal. The gunslinger let the hand-car coast slowly to a stop, and they peered around.

"It's like the subway," the boy said.

"Subway?"

"Never mind."

The boy climbed up and onto the hard cement. They looked at silent, deserted booths where newspapers and books had once been vended; an ancient bootery; a weapon shop (the gunslinger, with a sudden burst of excitement, saw revolvers and rifles; closer inspection showed that their barrels had been filled with lead; he did, however, pick out a bow, which he slung over his back, and a quiver of almost useless, badly weighted arrows); a women's apparel shop. Somewhere a converter was turning the air over and over, as it had for thousands of years — but perhaps not for much longer. It had a grating noise somewhere in the middle of its cycle which served to remind that perpetual motion, even under strictly controlled conditions, is still a fool's dream. The air had a mechanized taste. Their shoes made flat echoes.

The boy cried out: "Hey! Hey. . . . "

The gunslinger turned around and went to him. The boy was standing, transfixed, at the book stall. Inside, sprawled in the far corner, was a mummy. The mummy was wearing a blue uniform with gold piping — a trainman's uniform by the look. There was an ancient, perfectly preserved newspaper on the mummy's lap, which crumbled to dust when the gunslinger attempted to look at it. The mummy's face was like an old, shriveled apple. Cautiously, the gunslinger touched the cheek. There was a small puff of dust, and they looked through the cheek and into the mummy's mouth. A gold tooth twinkled.

"Gas," the gunslinger murmured. "They used to be able to make a gas that would do this."

"They fought wars with it," the boy said darkly.

"Yes."

There were other mummies, not a great many, but a few. They were all wearing blue and gold ornamental uniforms. The gunslinger supposed that the gas had been used when the place was empty of all incoming and outgoing traffic. Perhaps, in some dim day, the station had been a military objective of some long-gone army and cause.

The thought depressed him.

"We had better go on," he said, and started toward Track 10 and the handcar again. But the boy stood rebelliousy behind him.

"Not going."

The gunslinger turned back, surprised.

The boy's face was twisted and trembling. "You won't get what you want until I'm dead. I'll take my chances by myself."

The gunslinger nodded noncommitally, hating himself. "Okay." He turned around and walked across to the stone piers and leaped easily down onto the handcar.

"You made a deal!" The boy screamed after him. "I know you did!"

The gunslinger, not replying, carefully put the bow in front of the T-post rising out of the handcar's floor, out of harm's way.

The boy's fists were clenched, his features drawn in agony.

How easily you bluff this young boy, the gunslinger told himself dryly. Again and again his intuition has led him to this point, and again and again you have led him on by the nose — after all, he has no friends but you.

In a sudden, simple thought (almost a vision) it came to him that all he had to do was give it over, turn around, take the boy with him, make him the center of a new force. The Tower did not have to be obtained in this humiliating, nose-rubbing way. Let it come after the boy had a growth of years, when the two of them could cast the man in black aside like a cheap wind-up toy.

Surely, he thought cynically. Surely.

He knew with sudden coldness that going backward would mean death for both of them — death or worse: entombment with the living dead behind them. Decay of all the faculties. With, perhaps, the guns of his father living long after both of them, kept in rotten splendor as totems not unlike the unforgotten gas pump.

Show some guts, he told himself falsely.

He reached for the handle and began to pump it. The handcar moved away from the stone piers.

The boy screamed: *"Wait!"* And began running on the diagonal, toward where the handcar would emerge toward the darkness ahead. The gunslinger had an impulse to speed up, to leave the boy alone yet at least with an uncertainty.

Instead, he caught him as he leaped. The heart beneath

the thin shirt thrummed and fluttered as Jake clung to him.
It was like the beat of a chicken's heart.

It was very close now.

The sound of the river had become very loud, filling
even their dreams with its steady thunder. The gunslinger,
more as a whim than anything else, let the boy pump them
ahead while he shot a number of arrows into the dark, tethered by fine white lengths of thread.

The bow was very bad, incredibly preserved but with
a terrible pull and aim despite that, and the gunslinger
knew that very little would improve it. Even re-stringing
would not help the tired wood. The arrows would not fly
far into the dark, but the last one he sent out came back wet
and slick. The gunslinger only shrugged when the boy asked
him how far, but privately he didn't think the arrow could
have traveled more than a hundred yards from the rotted
bow — and lucky to get that.

And still the sound grew louder.

During the third waking period after the station, a
spectral radiance began to grow again. They had entered a
long tunnel of some weird phosphorescent rock, and the
wet walls glittered and twinkled with thousands of minute
starbursts. They saw things in a kind of eerie, horror-house
surreality.

The brute sound of the river was channeled to them by
the confining rock, magnified in its own natural amplifier.
Yet the sound remained oddly constant, even as they approached the crossing point the gunslinger was sure lay
ahead, because the walls were widening, drawing back. The
angle of their ascent became more pronounced.

The tracks arrowed straight ahead in the new light. To
the gunslinger they looked like the captive tubes of swamp

gas sometimes sold for a pretty at the Feast of Joseph fair-time; to the boy they looked like endless streamers of neon tubing. But in its glow they could both see that the rock that had enclosed them so long ended up ahead in ragged twin peninsulas that pointed toward a gulf of darkness ahead — the chasm over the river.

The tracks continued out and over the unknowable drop, supported by a trestle aeons old. And beyond, what seemed an incredible distance, was a tiny pinprick of light; not phosphorescence or fluorescence, but the hard, true light of day. It was as tiny as a needle-prick in a dark cloth, yet weighted with frightful meaning.

"Stop," the boy said. "Stop for a minute. Please."

Unquestioning, the gunslinger let the handcar coast to a rest. The sound of the river was a steady, booming roar, coming from beneath and ahead. The artificial glow from the wet rock was suddenly hateful. For the first time he felt a claustrophobic hand touch him, and the urge to get out, to get free of this living burial, was strong and nearly undeniable.

"We'll go through," the boy said. "Is that what he wants? For us to drive the handcar out over . . . that . . . and fall down?"

The gunslinger knew it was not but said: "I don't know what he wants."

"We're close now. Can't we walk?"

They got down and approached the lip of the drop carefully. The stone beneath their feet continued to rise until, with a sudden, angling drop, the floor fell away from the tracks and the tracks continued alone, across blackness.

The gunslinger dropped to his knees and peered down. He could dimly make out a complex, nearly incredible webwork of steel girders and struts, disappearing down

toward the roar of the river, all in support of the graceful
arch of the tracks across the void.

In his mind's eye he could imagine the work of time
and water on the steel, in deadly tandem. How much support was left? Little? Hardly any? None? He suddenly saw
the face of the mummy again, and the way the flesh, seemingly solid, had crumbled effortlessly to powder at the bare
touch of his finger.

"We'll walk," the gunslinger said.

He half expected the boy to balk again, but he preceded
the gunslinger calmly out onto the rails, crossing on the
welded steel slats calmly, with sure feet. The gunslinger
followed him, ready to catch him if Jake should put foot
wrong.

They left the handcar behind them and walked pre-
cariously out over darkness.

The gunslinger felt a fine slick of sweat cover his skin.
The trestle was rotten, very rotten. It thrummed beneath
his feet with the heady motion of the river far beneath,
swaying a little on unseen guy wires. We're acrobats, he
thought. Look, mother, no net. I'm flying. He knelt once
and examined the crossties they were walking on. They
were caked and pitted with rust (he could feel the reason
on his face; fresh air, the friend of corruption: very close
to the surface now), and a strong blow of the fist made the
metal quiver sickly. Once he heard a warning groan beneath
his feet and felt the steel settle preparatory to giving way,
but he had already moved on.

The boy, of course, was over a hundred pounds lighter
and safe enough, unless the going became progressively
worse.

Behind them, the handcar had melted into the general
gloom. The stone pier on the left extended out perhaps

twenty feet. Further than the one on the right, but this was also left behind and they were alone over the gulf.

At first it seemed that the tiny prick of daylight remained mockingly constant (perhaps drawing away from them at the exact pace they approached it — that would be wonderful magic indeed), but gradually the gunslinger realized that it was widening, becoming more defined. They were still below it, but the tracks were still rising.

The boy gave a surprised grunt and suddenly lurched to the side, arms pinwheeling in slow, wide revolutions. It seemed that he tottered on the brink for a very long time indeed before stepping forward again.

"It almost went on me," he said softly, without emotion. "Step over."

The gunslinger did so. The crosstie the boy had stepped on had given way almost entirely and flopped downward lazily, swinging easily on a disintegrating rivet, like a shutter on a haunted window.

Upward, still upward. It was a nightmare walk and so seemed to go on much longer than it did; the air itself seemed to thicken and become like taffy, and the gunslinger felt as if he might be swimming rather than walking. Again and again his mind tried to turn itself to thoughtful, lunatic consideration of the awful space between this trestle and the river below. His brain viewed it in spectacular detail, and how it would be: The scream of twisting metal, the lurch as his body slid off to the side, the grabbing for nonexistent handholds with the fingers, the swift rattle of bootheels on treacherous, rotted steel — and then down, turning over and over, the warm spray in his crotch as his bladder let go, the rush of wind against his face, rippling his hair up in cartoon fright, pulling his eyelids back, the dark water rushing to meet him, faster, outstripping even his own scream —

Metal screamed beneath him and he stepped past it unhurriedly, shifting his weight, not thinking of the drop, or of how far they had come, or of how far was left. Not thinking that the boy was expendable and that the sale of his honor was now, at last, nearly negotiated.

"Three ties out here," the boy said coolly. "I'm going to jump. Here! Here!"

The gunslinger saw him silhouetted for a moment against the daylight, an awkward, hunched spread-eagle. He landed and the whole edifice swayed drunkenly. Metal beneath them protested and something far below fell, first with a crash, then with the sound of deep water.

"Are you over?" The gunslinger asked.

"Yes," the boy said remotely, "but it's very rotten. I don't think it will hold you. Me, but not you. Go back now. Go back now and leave me alone."

His voice was hysterical, cold but hysterical.

The gunslinger stepped over the break. One large step did it. The boy was shuddering helplessly. "Go back. I don't want you to kill me."

"For Christ's sake, walk," the gunslinger said roughly. "It's going to fall down."

The boy walked drunkenly now, his hands held out shudderingly before him, fingers splayed.

They went up.

Yes, it was much more rotten now. There were frequent breaks of one, two, even three ties, and the gunslinger expected again and again that they would find the long empty space between rails that would either force them back or make them walk on the rails themselves, balanced giddily over the chasm.

He kept his eyes fixed on the daylight.

The glow had taken on a color — blue — and as it came closer it became softer, paling the radiance of the phosphor as it mixed with it. Fifty yards or a hundred? He could not say.

They walked, and now he looked at his feet, crossing from tie to tie. When he looked again, the glow had grown to a hole, and it was not a light but a way out. They were almost there.

Thirty yards, yes. Ninety short feet. It could be done. Perhaps they would have the man in black yet. Perhaps, in the bright sunlight the evil flowers in his mind would shrivel and anything would be possible.

The sunlight was blocked out.

He looked up, startled, staring, and saw a silhouette filling the light, eating it up, allowing only chinks of mocking blue around the outline of shoulders, the fork of crotch.

"Hello, boys!"

The man in black's voice echoed to them, amplified in this natural throat of stone, the sarcasm taking on mighty overtones. Blindly, the gunslinger sought the jawbone, but it was gone, lost somewhere, used up.

He laughed above them and the sound crashed around them, reverberating like surf in a filling cave. The boy screamed and tottered, a windmill again, arms gyrating through the scant air.

Metal ripped and sloughed beneath them; the rails canted through a slow and dreamy twisting. The boy plunged, and one hand flew up like a gull in the darkness, up, up, and then he hung over the pit; he dangled there, his dark eyes staring up at the gunslinger in final blind lost knowledge.

"Help me."

Booming, racketing: "Come now, gunslinger. Or catch me never!"

All chips on the table. Every card up but one. The boy dangled, a living Tarot card, the hanged man, the Phoeni-

cian sailor, innocent lost and barely above the wave of a
stygian sea.

Wait then, wait awhile.

"Do I go?" The voice so loud, he makes it hard to think,
the power to cloud men's minds. . . .

Don't make it bad, take a sad song and make it better. . . .

"Help me."

The trestle had begun to twist further, screaming, pulling loose from itself, giving —

"Then I shall leave you."

"No!"

His legs carried him in a sudden leap through the entropy that held him, above the dangling boy, into a skidding, plunging rush toward the light that offered, the Tower
frozen on the retina of his mind's eye in a black frieze, suddenly silence, the silhouette gone, even the beat of his heart
gone as the trestle settled further, beginning its final slow
dance to the depths, tearing loose, his hand finding the
rocky, lighted lip of damnation; and behind him, in the
dreadful silence, the boy spoke from too far beneath him.

"Go then. There are other worlds than these."

It tore away from him, the whole weight of it; and as he
pulled himself up and through to the light and the breeze
and the reality of a new karma *(we all shine on)*, he twisted his
head back, for a moment in his agony striving to be Janus
— but there was nothing, only plummeting silence, for the
boy made no sound.

Then he was up, pulling his legs through onto the rocky
escarpment that looked toward a grassy plain at the descending foot, toward where the man in black stood spread-legged,
with arms crossed.

The gunslinger stood drunkenly, pallid as a ghost, eyes
huge and swimming beneath his forehead, shirt smeared
with the white dust of his final, lunging crawl. It came to

him that he would always flee murder. It came to him that there would be further degradations of the spirit ahead that might make this one seem infinitesimal, and yet he would still flee it, down corridors and through cities, from bed to bed; he would flee the boy's face and try to bury it in cunts or even in further destruction, only to enter one final room and find it looking at him over a candle flame. He had become the boy; the boy had become him. He was a *wurderlak*, lycanthropus of his own making, and in deep dreams he would become the boy and speak strange tongues.

This is death. Is it? Is it?

He walked slowly, drunkenly down the rocky hill toward where the man in black waited. Here the tracks had been worn away, under the sun of reason, and it was as if they had never been.

The man in black pushed his hood away with the backs of both hands, laughing.

"So!" he cried. "Not an end, but the end of the beginning, eh? You progress, gunslinger! You progress! Oh, how I admire you!"

The gunslinger drew with blinding speed and fired twelve times. The gun-flashes dimmed the sun itself, and the pounding of the explosions slammed back from the rockfaced escarpments behind them.

"Now," the man in black said, laughing. "Oh, now. We make great magic together, you and I. You kill me no more than you kill yourself."

He withdrew, walking backwards, facing the gunslinger, grinning. "Come. Come. Come."

The gunslinger followed him in broken boots to the place of counseling.

THE
GUNSLINGER
AND THE
DARK MAN

he man in black led him to an ancient killing ground to make palaver. The gunslinger knew it immediately; a golgotha, place-of-the-skull. And bleached skulls stared blandly up at them — cattle, coyotes, deer, rabbits. Here the alabaster xylophone of a hen pheasant killed as she fed; there the tiny, delicate bones of a mole, perhaps killed for pleasure by a wild dog.

The golgotha was a bowl indented into the descending slope of the mountain, and below, in easier altitudes, the gunslinger could see Joshua trees and scrub firs. The sky overhead was a softer blue than he had seen for a twelve-month, and there was an indefinable something that spoke of the sea in the not-too-great distance.

I am in the West, Cuthbert, he thought wonderingly.

And of course in each skull, in each rondure of vacated eye, he saw the boy's face.

The man in black sat on an ancient ironwood log. His boots were powdered white with dust and the uneasy bone-meal of this place. He had put his hood up again, but the gunslinger could see the square shape of his chin clearly, and the shading of his jaw.

The shadowed lips twitched in a smile. "Gather wood, gunslinger. This side of the mountains is gentle, but at this altitude, the cold still may put a knife in one's belly. And this is a place of death, eh?"

"I'll kill you," the gunslinger said.

"No you won't. You can't. But you can gather wood to remember your Isaac."

The gunslinger had no understanding of the reference. He went wordlessly and gathered wood like a common cook's boy. The pickings were slim. There was no devil-grass on this side and the ironwood would not burn. It had become stone. He returned finally with a large armload, powdered and dusted with disintegrated bone, as if dipped in flour. The sun had sunk beyond the highest Joshua trees and had taken on a reddish glow and peered at them with baleful indifference through the black, tortured branches.

"Excellent," the man in black said. "How exceptional you are! How methodical! I salute you!" He giggled, and the gunslinger dropped the wood at his feet with a crash that ballooned up bone dust.

The man in black did not start or jump; he merely began laying the fire. The gunslinger watched, fascinated, as the idiogram (fresh, this time) took shape. When it was finished, it resembled a small and complex double chimney about two feet high. The man in black lifted his hand skyward, shaking back the voluminous sleeve from a tapered, handsome hand, and brought it down rapidly, index and pinky fingers forked out in the traditional sign of the evil eye. There was a blue flash of flame, and their fire was lighted.

"I have matches," the man in black said jovially, "but I thought you might enjoy the magic. For a pretty, gunslinger. Now cook our dinner."

The folds of his robe shivered, and the plucked and gutted carcass of a plump rabbit fell on the dirt.

The gunslinger spitted the rabbit wordlessly and roasted it. A savory smell drifted up as the sun went down.

Purple shadows drifted hungrily over the bowl where the man in black had chosen to finally face him. The gunslinger felt hunger begin to rumble endlessly in his belly as the rabbit browned; but when the meat was cooked and its juices sealed in, he handed the entire skewer wordlessly to the man in black, rummaged in his own nearly flat knapsack, and withdrew the last of his jerky. It was salty, painful to his mouth, and tasted like tears.

"That's a worthless gesture," the man in black said, managing to sound angry and amused at the same time.

"Nevertheless," the gunslinger said. There were tiny sores in his mouth, the result of vitamin deprivation, and the salt taste made him grin bitterly.

"Are you afraid of enchanted meat?"

"Yes."

The man in black slipped his hood back.

The gunslinger looked at him silently. In a way, the face of the man in black was an uneasy disappointment. It was handsome and regular, with none of the marks and twists which indicate a person who has been through awesome times and who has been privy to great and unknown secrets. His hair was black and of a ragged, matted length. His forehead was high, his eyes dark and brilliant. His nose was nondescript. The lips were full and sensual. His complexion was pallid, as was the gunslinger's own.

He said finally, "I expected an older man."

"Not necessary. I am nearly immortal. I could have taken a face that you more expected, of course, but I elected to show you the one I was — ah — born with. See, gunslinger, the sunset."

The sun had departed already, and the western sky was filled with a sullen furnace light.

"You won't see another sunrise for what may seem a very long time," the man in black said softly.

'The gunslinger remembered the pit under the mountains and then looked at the sky, where the constellations sprawled in clockspring profusion.

"It doesn't matter," he said softly, "now."

The man in black shuffled the cards with flying, merging rapidity. The deck was huge, the design on the backs of the cards convoluted. "These are tarot cards," the man in black was saying, "a mixture of the standard deck and a selection of my own development. Watch closely gunslinger."

"Why?"

"I'm going to tell your future, Roland. Seven cards must be turned, one at a time, and placed in conjunction with the others. I've not done this for over three hundred years. And I suspect I've never read one quite like yours." The mocking note was creeping in again, like a Kuvian night-soldier with a killing knife gripped in one hand. "You are the world's last adventurer. The last crusader. How that must please you, Roland! Yet you have no idea how close you stand to the Tower now, how close in time. Worlds turn about your head."

"Read my fortune then," he said harshly.

The first card was turned.

"The Hanged Man," the man in black said. The darkness had given him back his hood. "Yet here, in conjunction with nothing else, it signifies strength and not death. You, gunslinger, are the Hanged Man, plodding ever onward toward your goal over all the pits of Hades. You have already dropped one co-traveler into the pit, have you not?"

He turned the second card. "The Sailor. Note the clear brow, the hairless cheeks, the wounded eyes. He drowns, gunslinger, and no one throws out the line. The boy Jake."

The gunslinger winced, said nothing.

The third card was turned. A baboon stood grinningly

astride a young man's shoulder. The young man's face was turned up, a grimace of stylized dread and horror on his features. Looking more closely, the gunslinger saw the baboon held a whip.

"The Prisoner," the man in black said. The fire cast uneasy, flickering shadows over the face of the ridden man, making it seem to move and writhe in wordless terror. The gunslinger flicked his eyes away.

"A trifle upsetting, isn't he?" The man in black said, and seemed on the verge of sniggering.

He turned the fourth card. A woman with a shawl over her head sat spinning at a wheel. To the gunslinger's dazed eyes, she appeared to be smiling craftily and sobbing at the same time.

"The Lady of Shadows," the man in black remarked. "Does she look two-faced to you, gunslinger? She is. A veritable Janus."

"Why are you showing me these?"

"Don't ask!" The man in black said sharply, yet he smiled. "Don't ask. Merely watch. Consider this only pointless ritual if it eases you and cools you to do so. Like church."

He tittered and turned the fifth card.

A grinning reaper clutched a scythe with bony fingers. "Death," the man in black said simply. "Yet not for you."

The sixth card.

The gunslinger looked at it and felt a strange, crawling anticipation in his guts. The feeling was mixed with horror and joy, and the whole of the emotion was unnamable. It made him feel like throwing up and dancing at the same time.

"The Tower," the man in black said softly.

The gunslinger's card occupied the center of the pattern; each of the following four stood at one corner, like satellites circling a star.

"Where does that one go?" The gunslinger asked.

The man in black placed the Tower over the Hanged Man, covering it completely.

"What does that mean?" The gunslinger asked.

The man in black did not answer.

"What does that mean?" He asked raggedly.

The man in black did not answer.

"God damn you!"

No answer.

"Then what's the seventh card?"

The man in black turned the seventh. A sun rose in a luminously blue sky. Cupids and sprites sported around it.

"The seventh is Life," the man in black said softly. "But not for you."

"Where does it fit the pattern?"

"That is not for you to know," the man in black said. "Or for me to know." He flipped the card carelessly into the dying fire. It charred, curled and flashed to flame. The gunslinger felt his heart quail and turn icy in his chest.

"Sleep now," the man in black said carelessly. "Perchance to dream and that sort of thing."

"I'm going to choke you dead," the gunslinger said. His legs coiled with savage, splendid suddenness, and he flew across the fire at the other. The man in black, smiling, swelled in his vision and then retreated down a long and echoing corridor filled with obsidian pylons. The world filled with the sound of sardonic laughter, he was falling, dying, sleeping.

He dreamed.

The universe was void. Nothing moved. Nothing was.

The gunslinger drifted, bemused.

"Let us have light," the voice of the man in black said nonchalantly, and there was light. The gunslinger thought in a detached way that the light was good.

"Now darkness overhead with stars in it. Water down

below." It happened. He drifted over endless seas. Above, the stars twinkled endlessly.

"Land," the man in black invited. There was; it heaved itself out of the water in endless, galvanic convulsions. It was red, arid, cracked and glazed with sterility. Volcanoes blurted endless magma like giant pimples on some ugly adolescent's baseball head.

"Okay," the man in black was saying. "That's a start. Let's have some plants. Trees. Grass and fields."

There was. Dinosaurs rambled here and there, growling and whoofing and eating each other and getting stuck in bubbling, odiferous tarpits. Huge tropical rain-forests sprawled everywhere. Giant ferns waved at the sky with serated leaves. beetles with two heads crawled on some of them. All this the gunslinger saw. And yet he felt big.

"Now man," the man in black said softly, but the gunslinger was falling . . . falling up. The horizon of this vast and fecund earth began to curve. Yes, they had all said it had curved, his teachers, they had claimed it had been proved long before the world had moved on. But this —

Further and further. Continents took shape before his amazed eyes, and were obscured with clocksprings of clouds. The world's atmosphere held it in a placental sac. And the sun, rising beyond the earth's shoulder —

He cried out and threw an arm before his eyes.

"Let there be light!" The voice that cried was no longer that of the man in black. It was gigantic, echoing. It filled space, and the spaces between spaces.

"Light!"

Falling, falling.

The sun shrank. A red planet crossed with canals whirled past him, two moons circling it furiously. A whirling belt of stones. A gigantic planet that seethed with gasses, too huge to support itself, oblate in consequence. A ringed world that glittered with its engirdlement of icy spicules.

"Light! Let there be — "

Other worlds, one, two three. Far beyond the last, one lonely ball of ice and rock twirling in dead darkness about a sun that glittered no brighter than a tarnished penny.

Darkness.

"No," the gunslinger said, and his words were flat and echoless in the darkness. It was darker than dark. Beside it the darkest night of a man's soul was noonday. The darkness under the mountains was a mere smudge on the face of Light. "No more, please, no more now. No more — "

"LIGHT!"

"No more. No more, please — "

The stars themselves began to shrink. Whole nebulae drew together and became mindless smudges. The whole universe seemed to be drawing around him.

"Jesus no more no more no more — "

The voice of the man in black whispered silkily in his ear: "Then renege. Cast away all thoughts of the Tower. Go your way, gunslinger, and save your soul."

He gathered himself. Shaken and alone, enwrapt in the darkness, terrified of an ultimate meaning rushing at him, he gathered himself and uttered the final, flashing imperative:

"NO! NEVER!"

"THEN LET THERE BE LIGHT!"

And there was light, crashing in on him like a hammer, a great and primordial light. In it, consciousness perished — but before it did, the gunslinger saw something of cosmic importance. He clutched it with agonized effort and sought himself.

He fled the insanity the knowledge implied, and so came back to himself.

It was still night — whether the same or another, he had no way of knowing. He pushed himself up from where his demon spring at the man in black had carried him and looked at the ironwood where the man in black had been sitting. He was gone.

A great sense of despair flooded him — God, all that to do over again — and then the man in black said from behind him: "Over here, gunslinger. I don't like you so close. You talk in your sleep." He tittered.

The gunslinger got groggily to his knees and turned around. The fire had burned down to red embers and gray ashes, leaving the familiar decayed pattern of exhausted fuel. The man in black was seated next to it, smacking his lips over the greasy remains of the rabbit.

"You did fairly well," the man in black said. "I never could have sent that vision to Marten. He would have come back drooling."

"What was it?" The gunslinger asked. His words were blurred and shaky. He felt that if he tried to rise, his legs would buckle.

"The universe," the man in black said carelessly. He burped and threw the bones into the fire where they glistened with unhealthy whiteness. The wind above the cup of the golgotha whistled with keen unhappiness.

"Universe," the gunslinger said blankly.

"You want the Tower," the man in black said. It seemed to be a question.

"Yes."

"But you shan't have it," the man in black said, and smiled with bright cruelty. "I have an idea of how close to the edge that last pushed you. The Tower will kill you half a world away."

"You know nothing of me," the gunslinger said quietly, and the smile faded from the other's lips.

"I made your father and I broke him," the man in black said grimly. "I came to your mother through Marten and took her. It was written, and it was. I am the furthest minion of the Dark Tower. Earth has been given into my hand."

"What did I see?" The gunslinger asked. "At the end? What was it?"

"What did it seem to be?"

The gunslinger was silent, thoughtful. He felt for his tobacco, but there was none. The man in black did not offer to refill his poke by either black magic or white.

"There was light," the gunslinger said finally. "Great white light. And then — " He broke off and stared at the man in black. He was leaning forward, and an alien emotion was stamped on his face, writ too large for lies or denial. Wonder.

"You don't know," he said, and began to smile. "O great sorcerer who brings the dead to life. You don't know."

"I know," the man in black said. "But I don't know . . . what."

"White light," the gunslinger repeated. "And then — a blade of grass. One single blade of grass that filled everything. And I was tiny. Infinitesimal."

"Grass." The man in black closed his eyes. His face looked drawn and haggard. "A blade of grass. Are you sure?"

"Yes." The gunslinger frowned. "But it was purple."

And so the man in black began to speak.

The universe (he said) offers a paradox too great for the finite mind to grasp. As the living brain cannot conceive of a nonliving brain — although it may think it can — the finite mind cannot grasp the infinite.

The prosaic fact of the universe's existence single-handedly defeats the pragmatist and the cynic. There was a time, yet a hundred generations before the world moved on, when mankind had achieved enough technical and scientific prowess to chip a few splinters from the great stone pillar of reality. Even then, the false light of science (knowledge, if you like) shone in only a few developed countries.

Yet, despite a tremendous increase in available facts, there were remarkably few insights. Gunslinger, our fathers conquered the-disease-which-rots, which we call cancer, almost conquered aging, went to the moon —

("I don't believe that," the gunslinger said flatly, to which the man in black merely smiled and answered, "You needn't.")

— and made or discovered a hundred other marvelous baubles. But this wealth of information produced little or no insight. There were no great odes written to the wonders of artificial insemination —

("What?" "Having babies from frozen mansperm." "Bullshit." "As you wish . . . although not even the ancients could produce children from that material.")

— or to the car-which-moves. Few if any seemed to have grasped the Principle of Reality; new knowledge leads always to yet more awesome mysteries. Greater physiological knowledge of the brain makes the existence of the soul less possible yet more probable by the nature of the search. Do you see? Of course you don't. You are surrounded by your own romantic aura, you lie cheek and jowl daily with the arcane. Yet now you approach the limits — not of belief, but of comprehension. You face reverse entropy of the soul.

But to the more prosaic:

The greatest mystery the universe offers is not life but Size. Size encompasses life, and the Tower encompasses Size. The child, who is most at home with wonder, says: Daddy, what is above the sky? And the father says: The darkness of space. The child: What is beyond space? The father: The galaxy. The child: Beyond the galaxy? The father: Another galaxy. The child: Beyond the other galaxies? The father: No one knows.

You see? Size defeats us. For the fish, the lake in which

he lives is the universe. What does the fish think when he is jerked up by the mouth through the silver limits of existence and into a new universe where the air drowns him and the light is blue madness? Where hugh bipeds with no gills stuff it into a suffocating box and cover it with wet weeds to die?

Or one might take the point of a pencil and magnify it. One reaches the point where a stunning realization strikes home: The pencil point is not solid; it is composed of atoms which whirl and revolve like a trillion demon planets. What seems solid to us is actually only a loose net held together by gravitation. Shrunk to the correct size, the distances between these atoms might become leagues, gulfs, aeons. The atoms themselves are composed of nuclei and revolving protons and electrons. One may step down further to sub-atomic particles. And then to what? Tachyons? Nothing? Of course not. Everything in the universe denies nothing; to suggest conclusions to things is one impossibility.

If you fell outward to the limit of the universe, would you find a board fence and signs reading DEAD END? No. You might find something hard and rounded, as the chick must see the egg from the inside. And if you should peck through that shell, what great and torrential light might shine through your hole at the end of space? Might you look through and discover our entire universe is but part of one atom on a blade of grass? Might you be forced to think that by burning a twig you incinerate an eternity of eternities? That existence rises not to one infinite but to an infinity of them?

Perhaps you saw what place our universe plays in the scheme of things — as an atom in a blade of grass. Could it be that everything we can perceive, from the infinitesimal virus to the distant Horsehead Nebula, is contained in one blade of grass . . . a blade that may have existed for only a day or two in an alien time-flow? What if that blade should

be cut off by a scythe? When it began to die, would the rot seep into our own universe and our own lives, turning everything yellow and brown and desicated? Perhaps it's already begun to happen. We say the world has moved on; maybe we really mean that it has begun to dry up.

Think how small such a concept of things makes us, gunslinger! If a God watches over it all, does He actually mete out justice for a race of gnats among an infinitude of races of gnats? Does his eye see the sparrow fall when the sparrow is less than a speck of hydrogen floating disconnected in the depth of space? And if He does see . . . what must the nature of such a God be? Where does He live? How is it possible to live beyond infinity?

Imagine the sand of the Mohaine Desert, which you crossed to find me, and imagine a trillion universes — not worlds but universes — encapsulated in each grain of that desert; and within each universe an infinity of others. We tower over these universes from our pitiful grass vantage point; with one swing of your boot you may knock a billion billion worlds flying off into darkness, in a chain never to be completed.

Size, gunslinger . . . Size. . . .

Yet suppose further. Suppose that all worlds, all universes, met in a single nexus, a single pylon, a Tower. A stairway, perhaps, to the Godhead itself. Would you dare, gunslinger? Could it be that somewhere above all of endless reality, there exists a Room . . . ?

You dare not.

You dare not.

"Someone has dared," the gunslinger said.

"Who would that be?"

"God," the gunslinger said softly. His eyes gleamed. "God has dared . . . or is the room empty, seer?"

"I don't know." Fear passed over the man in black's

bland face, as soft and dark as a buzzard's wing. "And, furthermore, I don't ask. It might be unwise."

"Afraid of being struck dead?" The gunslinger asked sardonically.

"Perhaps afraid of an accounting," the man in black replied, and there was silence for a while. The night was very long. The Milky Way sprawled above them in great splendor, yet terrifying in its emptiness. The gunslinger wondered what he would feel if that inky sky should split open and let in a torrent of light.

"The fire," he said. "I'm cold."

The gunslinger drowsed and awoke to see the man in black regarding him avidly, unhealthily.

"What are you staring at?"

"You, of course."

"Well, don't." He poked up the fire, ruining the precision of the idiogram. "I don't like it." He looked to the east to see if there was the beginning of light, but this night went on and on.

"You seek the light so soon?"

"I was made for light."

"Ah, so you were! And so impolite of me to forget the fact! Yet we have much to discuss yet, you and I. For so has it been told to me by my master."

"Who?"

The man in black smiled. "Shall we tell the truth then, you and I? No more lies? No more glammer?"

"Glammer? What does that mean?"

But the man in black persisted: "Shall there be truth between us, as two men? Not as friends, but as enemies and equals? There is an offer you will get rarely, Roland. Only enemies speak the truth. Friends and lovers lie endlessly, caught in the web of duty."

"Then we'll speak the truth." He had never spoken

less on this night. "Start by telling me what glammer is."

"Glammer is enchantment, gunslinger. My master's enchantment has prolonged this night and will prolong it still . . . until our business is done."

"How long will that be?"

"Long. I can tell you no better. I do not know myself." The man in black stood over the fire, and the glowing embers made patterns on his face. "Ask. I will tell you what I know. You have caught me. It is fair; I did not think you would. Yet your quest has only begun. Ask. It will lead us to business soon enough."

"Who is your master?"

"I have never seen him, but you must. In order to reach the Tower you must reach this one first, the Ageless Stranger." The man in black smiled spitelessly. "You must slay him, gunslinger. Yet I think it is not what you wished to ask."

"If you've never seen him, how do you know him?"

"He came to me once in a dream. As a stripling he came to me, when I lived in a far land. A thousand years ago, or five or ten. He came to me in days before the old ones had yet to cross the sea. In a land called England. A sheaf of centuries ago he imbued me with my duty, although there were errands in between my youth and my apotheosis. You are that, gunslinger." He tittered. "You see, someone has taken you seriously."

"This Stranger has no name?"

"O, he is named."

"And what is his name?"

"Maerlyn," the man in black said softly, and somewhere in the easterly darkness where the mountains lay a rockslide punctuated his words and a puma screamed like a woman. The gunslinger shivered and the man in black flinched. "Yet I do not think that is what you wished to ask, either. It is not your nature to think so far ahead."

The gunslinger knew the question; it had gnawed him all this night, and he thought, for years before. It trembled on his lips but he didn't ask it . . . not yet.

"This Stranger, this Maerlyn, is a minion of the Tower? Like yourself?"

"Much greater than I. It has been given to him to live backward in time. He *darkles*. He *tincts*. He is in all times. Yet there is one greater than he."

"Who?"

"The Beast," the man in black whispered fearfully. "The keeper of the Tower. The originator of all *glammer*.

"What is it? What does this Beast — "

"Ask me no more!" The man in black cried. His voice aspired to sternness and crumbled into beseechment. "I know not! I do not wish to know. To speak of the Beast is to speak of the ruination of one's own soul. Before It, Maerlyn is as I am to him."

"And beyond the Beast is the Tower and whatever the Tower contains?"

"Yes," whispered the man in black. "But none of these things are what you wish to ask."

True.

"All right," the gunslinger said, and then asked the world's oldest question. "Do I know you? Have I seen you somewhere before?"

"Yes."

"Where?" The gunslinger leaned forward urgently. This was a question of his destiny.

The man in black clapped his hands to his mouth and giggled through them like a small child. "I think you know."

"Where!" He was on his feet; his hands had dropped to the worn butts of his guns.

"Not with those, gunslinger. Those do not open doors; those only close them forever."

"Where?" The gunslinger reiterated.

"Must I give him a hint?" The man in black asked the darkness. "I believe I must. "He looked at the gunslinger with eyes that burned. "There was a man who gave you advice," he said. "Your teacher — "

"Yes, Cort," the gunslinger interrupted impatiently.

"The advice was to wait. It was bad advice. For even then Marten's plans against your father had proceeded. And when your father returned — "

"He was killed," the gunslinger said emptily.

"And when you turned and looked, Marten was gone . . . gone west. Yet there was a man in Marten's entourage, a man who affected the dress of a monk and the shaven head of a penitent — "

"Walter," the gunslinger whispered. "You . . . you're not Marten at all. You're *Walter!*"

The man in black tittered. "At your service."

"I ought to kill you now."

"That would hardly be fair. After all, it was I who delivered Marten into your hands three years later, when — "

"Then you've controlled me."

"In some ways, yes. But no more, gunslinger. Now comes the time of sharing. Then, in the morning, I will cast the runes. Dreams will come to you. And then your real quest must begin."

"Walter," the gunslinger repeated, stunned.

"Sit," the man in black invited. "I tell you my story. Yours, I think, will be much longer."

"I don't talk of myself," the gunslinger muttered.

"Yet tonight you must. So that we may understand."

"Understand what? My purpose? You know that. To find the Tower.is my purpose. I'm sworn."

"Not your purpose, gunslinger. Your mind. Your slow, plodding, tenacious mind. There has never been one quite like it, in all the history of the world. Perhaps in the history of creation.

"This is the time of speaking. This is the time of histories."

"Then speak."

The man in black shook the voluminous arm of his robe. A foil-wrapped package fell out and caught the dying embers in many reflective folds.

"Tobacco, gunslinger. Would you smoke?"

He had been able to resist the rabbit, but he could not resist this. He opened the foil with eager fingers. There was fine crumbled tobacco inside, and green leaves to wrap it in, amazingly moist. He had not seen such tobacco for ten years.

He rolled two cigarettes and bit the ends of each to release flavor. He offered one to the man in black, who took it. Each of them took a burning twig from the fire.

The gunslinger lit his cigarette and drew the aromatic smoke deep into his lungs, closing his eyes to concentrate the senses. He blew out with long, slow satisfaction.

"Is it good?" the man in black enquired.

"Yes. Very good."

"Enjoy it. It may be the last smoke for you in a very long time."

The gunslinger took this impassively.

"Very well," the man in black said. "To begin then:

"You must understand that the Tower has always been, and there have always been boys who know of it and lust for it, more than power or riches or women. . . . "

There was talk then, a night's worth of talk and God alone knew how much more, but the Gunslinger remembered little of it later . . . and to his oddly practical mind, little of it seemed to matter. The man in black told him that he must go to the sea, which lay no more than twenty easy miles to the west, and there he would be invested with the power of *drawing*.

"But that's not exactly right, either," the man in black said, pitching his cigarette into the remains of the campfire. "No one wants to invest you with a power of any kind, gunslinger; it is simply in you, and I am compelled to tell you, partly because of the sacrifice of the boy, and partly because it is the law; the natural law of things. Water must run downhill, and you must be told. You will draw three, I understand . . . but I don't really care, and I don't really want to know."

"The three," the gunslinger murmured, thinking of the Oracle.

"And then the fun begins. But, by then, I'll be long gone. Good-bye, gunslinger. My part is done now. The chain is still in your hands. Beware it doesn't wrap itself around your neck."

Compelled by something outside him, Roland said, "You have one more thing to say, don't you?"

"Yes," the man in black said, and he smiled at the gunslinger with his depthless eyes and stretched one of his hands out toward him. "Let there be light."

And there was light.

Roland awoke by the ruins of the campfire to find himself ten years older. His black hair had thinned at the temples and gone the gray of cobwebs at the end of autumn. The lines in his face were deeper, his skin rougher.

The remains of the wood he had carried had turned to ironwood, and the man in black was a laughing skeleton in a rotting black robe, more bones in this place of bones, one more skull in golgotha.

The gunslinger stood up and looked around. He looked at the light and saw that the light was good.

With a sudden quick gesture he reached toward the remains of his companion of the night before . . . a night that had somehow lasted ten years. He broke off Walter's jawbone and jammed it carelessly into the left hip pocket of his jeans — a fitting enough replacement for the one lost under the mountains.

The Tower. Somewhere ahead, it waited for him — the nexus of Time, the nexus of Size.

He began west again, his back set against the sunrise, heading toward the ocean, realizing that a great passage of his life had come and gone. "I loved you, Jake," he said aloud.

The stiffness wore out of his body and he began to walk more rapidly. By that evening he had come to the end of the land. He sat on a beach which stretched left and right forever, deserted. The waves beat endlessly against the shore, pounding and pounding. The setting sun painted the water in a wide strip of fool's gold.

There the gunslinger sat, his face turned up into the fading light. He dreamed his dreams and watched as the stars came out; his purpose did not flag, nor did his heart falter; his hair, finer now and gray, blew around his head, and the sandalwood-inlaid guns of his father lay smooth and deadly against his hips, and he was lonely but did not find loneliness in any way a bad or ignoble thing. The dark came down on the world and the world moved on. The gun-slinger waited for the time of the *drawing* and dreamed his long dreams of the Dark Tower, to which he would some day come at dusk and approach, winding his horn, to do some unimaginable final battle.

AFTERWORD

The foregoing tale, which is almost (but not quite!) complete in itself, is the first stanza in a much longer work called *The Dark Tower*. Some of the work beyond this segment has been completed, but there is much more to be done — my brief synopsis of the action to follow suggests a length approaching 3000 pages, perhaps more. That probably sounds as if my plans for the story have passed beyond mere ambition and into the land of lunacy . . . but ask your favorite English teacher sometime to tell you about the plans Chaucer had for *The Canterbury Tales* — now *Chaucer* might have been crazy.

At the speed which the work entire has progressed so far, I would have to live approximately 300 years to complete the tale of the Tower; this segment, "The Gunslinger and the Dark Tower," was written over a period of twelve years. It is by far the longest I've taken with any work . . . and it might be more honest to put it another way: it is the longest that any of my unfinished works has remained alive and viable in my own mind, and if a book is not alive in the writer's mind, it is as dead as year-old horseshit even if words continue to march across the page.

The Dark Tower began, I think, because I inherited a ream of paper in the spring semester of my senior year in college. It wasn't a ream of your ordinary garden-variety bond paper, not even a ream of those colorful "second sheets" that many struggling writers use because those reams of colored sheets (often with large chunks of undissolved wood floating in them) are three or four dollars cheaper.

The ream of paper I inherited was bright green, nearly as thick as cardboard, and of an extremely eccentric size — about seven inches wide by about ten inches long, as I recall. I was working at the University of Maine library at the time, and several reams of this stuff, in various hues, turned up one day, totally unexplained and unaccounted for. My wife-to-be, the then Tabitha Spruce, took one of these reams of paper (robin's egg blue) home with her; the fellow she was then going with took home another (Roadrunner yellow). I got the green stuff.

As it happened, all three of us turned out to be real writers — a coincidence almost too large to be termed mere coincidence in a society where literally tens of thousands (maybe hundreds of thousands) of college students aspire to the writer's trade and where bare hundreds actually break through. I've gone on to publish half a dozen novels or so, my wife has published one *(Small World)* and is hard at work on an even better one, and the fellow she was going with back then, David Lyons, has developed into a fine poet and the founder of Lynx Press in Massachusetts.

Maybe it was the paper, folks. Maybe it was *magic* paper. You know, like in a Stephen King novel.

Anyway, all of you out there reading this may not understand how fraught with possibility those five hundred sheets of blank paper seemed to be, although I'd guess there are plenty of you who are nodding in perfect understanding right now. Publishing writers can, of course, have all the blank paper they want; it is their stock-in-trade. It's even tax deductable. They can have so much, in fact, that all of those blank sheets can actually begin to cast a malign spell — better writers than I have talked about the mute challenge

of all that white space, and God knows some of them have
been intimidated into silence by it.

The other side of the coin, particularly to a young writer, is almost unholy exhileration all that blank paper can
bring on; you feel like an alcoholic contemplating a fifth of
whiskey with the seal unbroken.

I was at that time living in a scuzzy riverside cabin not
far from the University, and I was living all by myself—
the first third of the foregoing tale was written in a ghastly,
unbroken silence which I now, with a houseful of rioting
children, two secretaries, and a housekeeper who always
thinks I look ill, find hard to remember. The three room-
mates with whom I had begun the year had all flunked out.
By March, when the ice went out of the river, I felt like the
last of Agatha Christie's ten little Indians.

Those two factors, the challenge of that blank green
paper, and the utter silence (except for the trickle of the
melting snow as it ran downhill and into the Stillwater),
were more responsible than anything else for the opening
lay of *The Dark Tower*. There was a third factor, but without
the first two, I don't believe the story ever would have been
written.

That third element was a poem I'd been assigned two
years earlier, in a sophomore course covering the earlier
romantic poets (and what better time to study romantic
poetry than in one's sophomore year?). Most of the other
poems had fallen out of my consciousness in the period
between, but that one, gorgeous and rich and inexplicable,
remained . . . and it remains still. That poem was "Childe
Roland," by Robert Browning.

I had played with the idea of trying a long romantic
novel embodying the feel, if not the exact sense, of the
Browning poem. Play was as far as things had gone because
I had too many other things to write — poems of my own,
short stories, newspaper columns, God knows what.

But during that spring semester, a sort of hush fell over my previously busy creative life—not a writer's block, but a sense that it was time to stop goofing around with a pick and shovel and get behind the controls of one big great God a'mighty steamshovel, a sense that it was time to try and dig something big out of the sand, even if the effort turned out to be an abysmal failure.

And so, one night in March of 1970, I found myself sitting at my old office-model Underwood with the chipped 'm' and the flying capital 'O' and writing the words that begin this story: *The man in black fled across the desert and the gunslinger followed.*

In the years since I typed that sentence, with Johnny Winter on the stereo not quite masking the sound of melting snow running downhill outside, I have started to go gray, I have begotten children, I have buried my mother, I have gone on drugs and gone off them, and I've learned a few things about myself — some of them rueful, some of them unpleasant, most of them just plain funny. As the gunslinger himself would probably point out, the world has moved on.

But I've never completely left the gunslinger's world in all that time. The thick green paper got lost somewhere along the way, but I still have the original forty or so pages of typescript, comprising the sections titled "The Gunslinger" and "The Way Station." It was replaced by a more legitimate-looking paper, but I remember those funny green sheets with more affection than I could ever convey in words. I came back to the gunslinger's world when 'Salem's Lot was going badly ("The Oracle and the Mountains") and wrote of the boy Jake's sad ending not long after I had seen another boy, Danny Torrance, escape another bad place in *The Shining*. In fact, the only time when my thoughts did not turn at least occasionally to the gunslinger's dry and yet somehow gorgeous world (at least it has always seemed gorgeous to me) was when I was inhabiting another that seemed every bit as real—the post-apocalypse world of *The Stand.* The final segment presented here, "The Gunslinger and the Man in Black," was written less than eighteen months ago, in western Maine.

I believe that I probably owe readers who have come this far with me some sort of synopsis ("the argument," those great old romantic poets would have called it) of what is to come, since I'll almost surely die before completing the entire novel . . . or epic . . . or whatever you'd call it. The sad fact is that I can't really do that. People who know me understand that I am not an intellectual ball of fire, and people who have read my work with some critical approval (there are a few; I bribe them) would probably agree that the best of my stuff has come more from the heart than from the head . . . or from the gut, which is the place from which the strongest emotional writing originates.

All of which is just a way of saying that I'm never completely sure where I'm going, and in this story that is even more true than usual. I know from Roland's vision near the end that his world is indeed moving on because Roland's universe exists within a single molecule of a weed dying in some cosmic vacant lot (I think I probably got this idea from Clifford D. Simak's *Ring Around the Sun;* please don't sue me, Cliff!), and I know that the *drawing* involves calling three people from our own world (as Jake himself was called by the man in black) who will join Roland in his quest for the Dark Tower—I know that because segments of the second cycle of stories (called "The Drawing of the Three") have already been written.

But what of the gunslinger's murky past? God, I know so little. The revolution that topples the gunslinger's "world of light"? I don't know. Roland's final confrontation with Marten, who seduces his mother and kills his father? Don't know. The deaths of Roland's compatriots, Cuthbert and

Jamie, or his adventures during the years between his coming of age and his first appearance to us in the desert? I don't know that, either. And there's this girl, Susan. Who is she? Don't know.

Except somewhere inside, I do. Somewhere inside I know all of those things, and there is no need of an argument, or a synopsis, or an outline (outlines are the last resource of bad fiction writers who wish to God they were writing masters' theses). When it's time, those things—and their relevance to the gunslinger's quest—will roll out as naturally as tears or laughter. And if they never get around to rolling out, well, as Confucious once said, five hundred million Red Chinese don't give a shit.

I do know this: at some point, at some magic time, there will be a purple evening (an evening made for romance!) when Roland will come to his dark tower, and approach it, winding his horn . . . and if I should ever get there, you'll be the first to know.

Stephen King
Bangor, Maine